Bloodlines AND Betrayals

A MAFIA ROMANCE

Lorraine Carey

Copyright 2026 by Lorraine Carey

All rights reserved.

No part of this book may be reproduced or transmitted in any form or by any means, electronic or mechanical, including photocopying, recording, or by any information storage and retrieval system, without permission in writing from the author or publisher except in the case of brief quotations embodied in critical articles or reviews.

ISBN: 978-1-970730-84-5

Visit my blog:

authorlorrainecarey.blogspot.com

AUTHOR'S NOTE

The Connection

This book is more than just fiction — it is a reflection of a lifelong connection. I was born and raised in a suburb of Youngstown, Ohio, a place that offered a vibrant and formative backdrop to my youth. The memories I carry of its neighborhoods, clubs, and gathering places from my high school and college years have stayed with me, ultimately inspiring the story you now hold in your hands.

Youngstown has long been known for many things, including the complex history of organized crime that shaped parts of its reputation. Yet to me, it was also a city alive with energy and possibility — a cultural crossroads where people from many backgrounds came together to build lives, families, and community. During the 1960s and early 1970s, it thrived as a true melting pot, fueled in large part by the steel mills that drew hardworking immigrants, including my own grandparents, to its streets and neighborhoods.

While certain locations and street names in this story are drawn from real places, the characters and events are entirely fictional and created for entertainment. Still, the spirit of the town — the resilience, the diversity, and the memories that shaped me — remains deeply woven into these pages.

It is my hope that readers will feel the authenticity and affection behind this work and sense the personal bond that inspired its creation.

Enjoy the story.

Acknowledgments

I want to thank my beta reader, Becky Robbins, whose invaluable insights shaped the ending of this story and made it so memorable.

Chapter 1

1976

Elena Donato burst through the front door, cheeks flushed from more than the cold night air. The door slammed shut behind her with a thud that echoed through the quiet house.

The familiar scent of coffee and vanilla wrapped around her like a childhood memory. In the country-style kitchen, her mother sat at the table, fingers curled around a half-empty mug, eyes sharp despite the late hour, as if she'd been waiting for Elena to arrive home.

"Ma!" Elena whipped off her red beret, sending her long raven hair tumbling over her faded jean jacket. She dropped into the chair across from her mother, practically vibrating. "You won't believe what happened tonight!"

Francesca, otherwise known as Fran, lifted one perfectly shaped brow and set down her mug with delicate care. "Try me."

"I've met the hottest guy I've ever seen!" Elena grinned, eyes sparkling. "Tall. Dark. Ridiculously handsome. And he asked for my number — said he would call me tomorrow.

She studied her daughter the way a general assesses a battlefield. "And where," she asked slowly, "did you meet this miracle?"

"At The Steel Edge." Elena hesitated just a beat. "Pam and I were about to leave — the place was dead. Then he walked in and asked me to dance. The band was playing their last number, Ma." She leaned closer, lowering her voice. "And he's Italian."

The air in the kitchen shifted.

Fran's fingers tightened around her mug. "Italian," she repeated flatly. "How many times do I have to tell you to stay away from that club?"

"Ma —"

"That place is owned by men who ruin lives," Fran snapped, eyes blazing." People just don't hang out there, Elena. They're connected. All of them."

"I don't even know if he is," Elena said, standing next to the kettle. "You're jumping to conclusions."

Her mother followed her, her shadow long under the kitchen light. "What's his name?"

Elena didn't face her mother. "Tony. Tony Marinetti."

The mug slipped from Fran's hand, shattering against the linoleum, porcelain exploding like a gunshot in a quiet house.

"Marinetti?" she whispered.

Elena knelt, startled. "Yeah ... yeah, Marinetti." She reached for the shards.

Fran pressed a paper towel into her daughter's hand, her face drained of color. "Madone!" she breathed. "Not them."

"What's wrong?" Elena asked, irritation creeping in. "You're acting as if the devil himself asked me to dance."

"Because he might as well have. "The Marinettis are a mob family. And not the good kind."

Elena's eyes narrowed. "Oh, and what's the good kind, Ma? The ones you come from?"

"Sit," Her mother ordered.

She poured herself fresh coffee, hands trembling just enough to notice, then lowered her voice. "Your father's asleep."

Elena sat, arms crossed, curiosity burning now. Petite and silver-haired, Fran looked fragile to strangers. Those who knew better understood the fire beneath the calm.

"You figured out our history years ago," Fran said quietly. "We had that talk."

"I figured it out because I'm smart," Elena replied. "And because you whisper when you think I'm not listening."

Despite herself, Fran smiled faintly. "My cousin, Lamberto, "The Lamb" as they call him — he's still active. Cleveland, Chicago, Pittsburgh."

Elena scoffed. "That nickname has always been a joke. And you're saying he's better than the Marinettis because …?"

"Different family. Different rules." Francesca took a careful sip. "Lamberto specializes in things best left unseen." Her voice dropped. "Our families didn't part on good terms. You're not just risking yourself — you're risking all of us."

"You're assuming way too much," Elena said, standing. "You don't know Tony. And if he calls, I'm going."

She paused halfway up the stairs. "Goodnight, Ma."

Her mother didn't answer.

She dumped her cold coffee down the sink, the dark liquid spiraling away. *Salvatore will never forgive me*, she thought. He'd barely accepted her past as it was.

She stopped at the small table beneath the stairs, crowded with candles and statues. The Virgin Mary stood watch in the center.

"Protect her," she whispered. "Please."

Because somewhere deep down, she knew …

If Tony Marinetti called, it was only the beginning.

Chapter 2

Elena was glad to slip into her comfy nightgown and climb into bed. Her thoughts shifted from anger to excitement at the thought of Tony phoning her. *Mob or no mob, I don't care; he's hot! Oh, the way he strutted in with those black Ray-Bans and a black leather jacket. And the way he acted as though he owned the place. It seemed as though people froze when he entered the club.* Visions of his jet-black hair slicked back behind his ears filled her thoughts. With that, she drifted off to a deep sleep.

Sunlight peeked through the thin blinds, waking her. She glanced over at her clock and saw it was now 8:30. Since it was Saturday, she had no classes at the university. She relished the fact that she could sleep in. She threw on her robe and headed downstairs for a cup of tea. She knew her parents would most likely be awake and have already had breakfast. Both were early risers.

Elena tiptoed down the stairs but stopped on the first landing as she heard her mom speaking in a loud tone to her father. "Salvatore, I don't know what we'll do if she goes out with this gangster! You and I both know the Marinetti family, and we know what happened seven years ago. They are bad news."

"Yes, I remember it well. It's one memory I try to suppress, but I love you and accept who you are, despite your family's past actions. Now, calm down, Fran. She hasn't even had a date yet. Let's take things one step at a time," Salvatore said, pouring himself another cup of coffee.

Elena clenched her fists and froze at what she heard. *How dare they! I'm twenty-two years old and well capable of making my own decisions. This isn't the old country!* She knew she had to calm down before she headed into the kitchen.

"Good morning, sweetheart!" Salvatore chirped as he rose from his chair to hug his daughter.

Elena kissed him on the cheek and then turned to kiss her mother as well.

"Your mom tells me you have met a handsome young man."

Elena sat down as her mom turned the kettle on for her tea. "Yes, I have. I'm sure Mother has told you all about him."

"Not so much. I would love to hear about it, that's if you want to talk about it." Salvatore wanted to hear the words from his daughter even though he'd been versed by Fran.

Elena shrugged her shoulders and proceeded to tell her father how she met him and that he was supposed to call her.

To her surprise, her father responded quite cheerfully. "I'm happy for you. I hope he *does* call, and I hope he knows how lucky he is if you accept an offer for a date."

Fran sat there, slack-jawed. Her husband wasn't as upset as she was. He was not a worrier like her and had more of a laid-back attitude.

"Well, we will see if he calls," Elena responded as her mom poured her a cup of tea.

"Any plans for today?" her mother asked.

"Not much. I'm going to call Pam and see if she wants to go to the mall and do some shopping for new outfits for spring."

"Now that sounds like fun. Your father and I have some shopping to do ourselves, so we may be out the rest of the day."

Elena was glad her mother didn't bring up anything else regarding Tony. She finished her toast and tea and headed up to her room to call Pam.

Pam answered on the first ring, excited to talk to her friend. She wanted to rehash all the details from last night at the club and the hot Italian guy. "Do you think he'll call you?" she asked.

"I hope so. He's all I could think about, but if it's up to my mother, she'll do anything in her power to keep me from seeing him."

"What ... why?"

"She thinks his family is the mob — the bad kind."

"Is there a good kind?" Pam asked.

"Very funny," Elena replied, not wanting to go into any details about her mother's family. She was pretty sure Pam's family had no ties, but everyone in Youngstown was aware of the mob and all the businesses they used as a cover for their illegal organizations.

Pam declined Elena's offer because she had to visit her aunt, but wanted firsthand details if Tony did call.

Elena decided to shower and then head to the mall herself. Maybe that would take her mind off Tony for a while.

Just as she hopped out of the shower, she heard the phone ringing. She wrapped a towel around herself and headed to the phone in the upstairs hallway. Her heart skipped a beat when she heard Tony's velvety voice. She was glad her parents had already left the house, so she didn't have to whisper.

"Elena ... are you there?" Tony asked in a low voice, noting there was no answer yet.

"Yes ... I'm here. How are you?"

"I'm good, but I'd be even better if you would join me tonight for dinner at Rossini's. You know it's the best Italian restaurant in the area."

Elena paused again, her heart racing. "Sure, I'd love to."

"How about I pick you up, say, around sevenish? I need to know your address."

"It's ... it's ..."

Elena sat down on the floor in the hallway, contemplating the backlash she would get from her mother if he came to the house.

"Is something wrong, Elena?" he asked.

"No, no. It's fine." She rambled off her address quickly and decided to face the fray this evening.

"Aw, so Struthers it is. I'm familiar with that area." He proceeded to tell her he was looking forward to their date before he ended the call.

Elena set the phone back in its cradle and headed into her bedroom in a daze. *Now I just have to figure out what to wear and how to break the news to Mom.* Her shopping trip had to be put on hold; there was too much to do now, too much to think about.

She heard the garage door opening. She flew into a panic mode as she rushed downstairs to help her parents unload groceries. *Maybe I can butter Mom up before I break the news of my date tonight,* she thought as she carried two heavy bags into the kitchen.

"Well, someone seems to be in a good mood," her mother said, plopping down a large bag filled with produce. "Oh ... don't tell me that mafioso's son called you!"

Elena took a deep breath and readied herself for some heavy repercussions from her mother. "Actually, he did. And I'm so excited I could burst!"

Her mother shook her head and turned to Salvatore, who had just brought in the last of the groceries. "What are we going to do? We can't allow that gangster to come here!"

Salvatore took his wife's hand and instructed her to sit down. Elena's heart began to race as she stood by the kitchen sink, waiting to hear what her father had to say.

"Now listen, Fran, you don't have any real evidence that this young man is involved in crime like his father. Let her go out with him. I mean, it's just one night. Who knows, this may never lead to anything serious."

Fran's face was beet red. "It better not, because we can't have our family name tainted."

"Oh, you mean your family name," Salvatore said as he shook his head. "I believe that's already been taken care of."

Fran's eyes shot daggers at her husband.

Elena hugged her dad. "Thanks for sticking up for him. I have a feeling this guy is clean and not the thug Mom makes him out to be." She pulled away, still hanging onto his muscular arms, locking her eyes with his deep browns.

"Now let's hear the details of this date tonight," he inquired as he began to unpack the groceries.

Fran held her words as she wanted to hear all the details before she commented.

Elena told them that Tony was taking her to Rossini's. "He'll be here at 7 p.m."

"Rossini's ... huh?" Fran shook her head.

"Yes, you know they are supposed to have great Italian food," Elena added.

"A known mob-run business," Fran added in a snarky tone.

"Enough!" Salvatore held up his hands, indicating for his wife to stop. But she kept mumbling under her breath about the mob and went about unpacking groceries.

Elena offered to help, but both her folks declined her offer, telling her to spend the day getting ready for her date.

Elena padded out of the kitchen and headed up the stairs, relieved that the initial announcement was over, but she stopped at the first landing to overhear her mother's voice.

"I'm going to have to call Lamberto. He's got to follow them. I don't like anything about this."

"Look, you're making matters worse, Fran! By God, your cousin is still an active hitman. You planning to take this kid out? There's no reason to get him involved. It's just a date." Salvatore stood blocking the yellow kitchen wall phone.

Elena felt ill. She knew her mom's cousin was in the mob, had heard rumors but didn't know how much Lamberto was involved. She walked up to her room and sat on her bed. Her head pounded, and her heart raced. She had to lie down for a bit to get her composure.

A gentle knock on her bedroom door woke her from a quick nap. It was her mom. She sat on the bed and apologized to Elena, telling her she knew she was being overprotective, but she worried for her safety.

"So, your cousin won't be following us?" Elena asked. "I had no idea he was a killer!"

Fran shook her head and took hold of Elena's hand. "Look, he had a one-time run-in with a hardcore criminal from Cleveland who was a threat to our family. We vowed to protect one another. It's how we roll."

"And you're okay now with me going out with Tony?"

"Not so much, but your father convinced me it should be okay," she said. "I just want you to know what you're dealing with here. Once you get involved with this type of family, your reputation will be tarnished, and people will never see you in the same light. This is a small town. Trust me. I don't want to have to say, *I told you so.*" Fran squared her shoulders and headed toward the door.

As soon as she shut her door, Elena took a deep breath and then rummaged through her closet in search of something to wear tonight, with thoughts of having a hitman in her family still racing in her brain. She had hours to prepare but knew she'd most likely spend too much time worrying about what to wear.

She pulled a red miniskirt and a white ruffled blouse up to herself, looking in her dresser mirror. *This seems sexy but not too inappropriate. Now, to do something with my hair.*

She styled her long hair in a high ponytail with a red ribbon to match her skirt and applied red lipstick to give it the final touch. Checking herself in the mirror, Elena was finally satisfied with the way she looked. She grabbed her short, white leather jacket before heading downstairs. Late April meant the evenings were still cool. The minutes ticked away.

Having her folks meet Tony was a given, and with that thought, her stomach had a few knots. She headed downstairs to show off her outfit to her folks, twirling around to get their approval.

Her father smiled, and her mom gave a half-smile. "That skirt is a bit short," her mom added.

"Well, it's the 70s, Mom. It's a miniskirt, and this is the look," Elena added.

Her mother gave her a disapproving look. "I guess so, but you're sending this guy the wrong message."

The sound of a loud car engine pulling into the driveway brought the conversation to an end. Elena peeked out the front window to see a red Mustang GT pull in. "He's here!" she cheered.

Elena opened the door to find Tony decked out in black denims and his signature black leather jacket, minus the Ray-Bans. He waited to be invited in.

Stepping into the house, his eyes glanced around the country-style furniture in the living room. "Very nice," he said, smoothing his hair back.

"Thank you. My mom has a knack for this type of thing," she said, taking his hand and leading him into the kitchen. She took a deep breath, knowing her parents were patiently waiting to meet him.

Tony was most gracious as he reached his hand out to shake both her parents' hands. He even complimented Francesca. "You have some great taste when it comes to decorating."

With that, Fran thanked him and asked them what their plans were, knowing what they were but wanting to hear it from him, causing Elena's face to turn red with embarrassment.

Tony mentioned Rossini's, and Fran had to search for words. "Well ... I hope you enjoy the food."

Elena blew a kiss to her parents as she and Tony turned to head to the front door.

As soon as she heard a car door slam, Fran peered out the front window. "Look, there's a black Town Car parked in the street. It's his dad's bodyguards!"

"Calm down now, Fran. You're getting yourself worked up," Salvatore said, standing right behind her.

"I can't calm down. She's going out with a mobster's son! I've got to call Lamberto!"

"No, not the Lamb!" shouted Salvatore, mocking her, his hands in the air.

* * *

Tony complimented Elena on her hairstyle. She smoothed her long ponytail and thanked him. "I wanted to look nice for you."

"Darlin, you could come in a shower curtain and look fantastic."

Um ... did he really say a shower curtain? She chuckled to herself.

It wasn't until they turned onto Youngstown Poland Road that she noticed the black Town Car following them. Alarmed, Elena turned to Tony. "Who are those guys following us?"

"Oh, those dudes ... they are friends of my dad. Just making sure this car doesn't break down. I've been having issues with it, and you know how hard it is to get a mechanic on the weekend."

Hmm ... don't know if I believe that one, Elena thought, remembering what her mom had said.

"Everything okay?" Tony asked, aware of Elena's silence.

"Yes, it's all good, Tony. Guess I'm just nervous for some reason."

"You don't have to be, darlin'. Not when you're with me."

Tony turned up the volume as Bruce Springsteen singing "Born to Run" came on the radio. He turned to Elena. "I love this song!"

Elena agreed and scooted closer to him, flashing a smile while wondering what exactly he meant by that statement.

The valets at the restaurant seemed to be awaiting their arrival. Two young men opened the car doors for them. Tony came around to take Elena's hand as a tall, uniformed doorman greeted Tony like he was the king of a faraway land.

Elena turned around to see if the Town Car was still there. She didn't see it, but was too excited and let that thought go.

A tall older man holding two menus led them to a table in the far back. The low lighting and candles glowing on the tables made for a romantic atmosphere.

Tony pulled the chair out for Elena. He was quite the gentleman.

Taking a seat, he leaned in to take her hand, "Get anything you want tonight. It's all on the house. Get the best wine and whatever you want."

* * *

Ignoring her husband's request, Fran called Lamberto, luckily reaching him on the second ring. "And what do I owe the honor of this call, cousin?"

"It's Elena."

"What's wrong? Is she okay?" Lamberto's voice was full of alarm.

"She's okay, but I need your help. She's out on a date with Ralph Marinetti's son."

"You don't say. Now, how in the hell did that happen?"

"She met him at a club the other night. She won't listen to me about how dangerous this is. You know how stubborn she is."

"Yes, just like someone else I know," Lamberto said jokingly. "I do know the ramifications this can have for our family. I'm sure she has no idea I shot his dad's cousin long ago. We're still in dangerous times. Let me know where they went, and I'll be glad to take a drive by and check on her."

"She's at Rossini's."

"Aw, yes, one of Marinetti's businesses. I get it."

Fran was relieved and thanked her cousin. He promised to give her a call when he got home to report anything suspicious.

She turned to find Salvatore standing there with his arms crossed over his chest, shaking his head.

* * *

The glow from the candle that graced the center of the table illuminated Tony's olive complexion and full lips. Elena couldn't help but feel her attraction to this handsome man.

Tony lit a cigarette, took a puff, and reached for Elena's hand. "You know I have to tell you how sexy you look tonight in that miniskirt. It's hard for a man like me to control himself from taking you right out to the car and having my way with you."

Elena's eyes got as big as saucers, not knowing how to respond. His words were turning her on in ways she hadn't experienced before.

After ordering chicken parmesan for her and Tony's lobster ravioli, they sipped the expensive wine the waiter kept pouring.

The cook made an appearance at the table to see how the food was and gave a wink to Tony, which was not missed by Elena.

Unbeknownst to Elena, Lamberto was cruising the restaurant parking lot. He caught sight of the black Town Car with two of Ralph Marinetti's henchmen and knew they also noticed him. They were all there to provide protection, but for different people. Lamberto parked at the far end of the lot.

Tony and Elena walked arm in arm out of the restaurant. Elena's mind was too preoccupied with her feelings to worry about the Town Car that had been following them. Nor did she notice Lamberto's silver Cutlass Supreme. He had his binoculars out, scoping out the couple. His usual fedora covered most of his face, but those who knew him knew it was his signature look. With a face that resembled a pit bull, many people knew not to mess with him.

On the short drive home, Tony placed his hand between Elena's legs. She turned to see him with a huge grin on his face. He expressed his desire to invite her out again next weekend, and she readily accepted.

* * *

Fran was startled by the late-night phone call, and her heart raced when she heard Lamberto's voice on the other end. "I saw the car!"

"What? Whose car?"

"A black Town Car that belongs to Ralph Marinetti's guys. There were two men inside. I also spotted Tony's car. I waited until they came out of the restaurant. He was holding her close as they walked to the car."

Fran had no words, trying to control herself. "See, it's just as I thought. Ralph's son is dangerous, and now he's got my daughter involved as well."

"Not to worry, cousin. I'll be vigilant in this situation. Familia always comes first."

Fran twisted and turned as she tried to relax in the overstuffed chair in her bedroom until she heard the door open and knew it was Elena returning home. She breathed a sigh of relief knowing her daughter was safe, but for how long?

Chapter 3

Elena jumped up, realizing she'd slept in. She had wanted to go to an early Mass with her parents, but it was 9 a.m., and she'd never make it in time. Throwing on her robe, she headed downstairs, trailing the scent of strong coffee. Her mom had left a note indicating they'd gone to Mass and she should relax and enjoy the omelet in the fridge.

After pouring herself a cup of coffee, she warmed up the omelet and toasted a slice of bread. Her appetite was in full swing, as well as her hormones. She sat and thought about last night's date with Tony. She thought about how his hand felt on her leg, and she hoped there would be another date. But she had to get through her mother first, and that would take some effort.

Her only plans for the day were to catch up on research for her art class and meet Pam to have a girl chat. After finishing her breakfast, she called Pam and made plans to meet at the Coffee Corner for lunch.

Her parents had arrived home from church and were anxious to hear about her date. Elena indulged in a second cup of coffee as her mom put on a fresh pot. She figured maybe more caffeine would put her in a more talkative mood.

"Dinner was delicious, but not as good as yours," she said as she hugged her mom.

"Yeah, now don't try to butter me up. You know I wasn't in favor of you going out with that mobster's son last night," Fran said, shaking her head.

Elena stood back, "I don't want to get into any of this with you now. I had a great time, and if you love me, you'll want me to be happy."

Salvatore came up and hugged his daughter. "Of course, we do, darling. Your mother is just being your mother."

Elena inhaled a deep breath, excusing herself to shower and get dressed for her lunch date with Pam.

Fran waited until Elena was out of earshot and turned to her husband, "Well, at least Pam is safe territory."

"You know, you're on the right track if you're aiming to distance yourself from our daughter," Salvatore said, putting his hand on his wife's shoulder. "I won't stand for this. I know you have your reasons, but let's let her live her life."

Fran turned around quickly, "It's what I want most for her — to live!"

With that, Salvatore left to do some outside yard work, and Fran carried on with house chores. She planned to contact Lamberto later and get more details.

Coffee Corner was empty for a Sunday morning. Elena took a table in the back by the window and watched for Pam's car to pull up.

As Pam entered the café, Elena rose and motioned to her.

Pam always looked stunning, whether she was going casual or in club wear. Her blonde shag haircut and green silk scarf made her the epitome of the new disco look, which was all the rage now. The girls exchanged hugs, removed their jackets, and sat down. The waitress dashed over with the menus, and both girls ordered Cokes to start.

Pam leaned across the table. "Well, tell me about your date. I've been dying to talk to you!"

Pam listened with rapt attention as Elena filled her in on all the details. "Is he gonna call you again?"

"I pray so, but I've got that mom issue, as you know."

"Yeah, I do know, and I'm sorry about that," Pam said, taking her friend's hand.

"She thinks I'm going to end up kidnapped, or dead, for that matter."

"Well, it's far-fetched, but it has happened in this town," Pam said, glancing out the window.

Elena noticed Pam kept her eyes on the window. "What's out there?"

"Not sure, but two men in long black coats and black hats just got out of a new black Town Car. Looks like they're going to a funeral."

Elena's eyes shot to the door as the two middle-aged men entered and took seats at the counter. They both removed their hats. One man was balding, and the other had a thick head of black curly hair.

Pam whispered to Elena, "See, those are the guys!"

"Yeah, but I think you're just being paranoid.

When the bald one turned to stare at the girls, Pam noticed a long scar on the right side of his face and felt a surge of alarm. "We should get out of here. These guys give me the creeps. Didn't you say you saw a Town Car following you last night?"

"Yes, but it was nothing. You're beginning to sound like my mother. But if you feel uneasy, we can leave and go to my house," Elena suggested. My mom is always glad to see you."

Both men turned to watch the girls as they sauntered out the door.

Pam stood by her car before she got in. "See what I mean, I think they *are* following us. Did you see the way they stared at us as we walked by?"

Elena just shook her head and told her friend she'd meet her at her house.

Chapter 4

Tony was happy to catch his dad before he left for work. He wanted to ask him about his schedule for the day, knowing it changed quite frequently, and Mondays were usually full.

His dad was just finishing his coffee as Miss Ginny, their maid, was cleaning off the table. Tony took a seat next to his dad, and Miss Ginny asked if he wanted something to eat. He thanked her and declined the offer, adding he was heading out soon.

Ralph Marinetti was a man of many secrets, and even ones he had to keep from his maid, who was always lurking. He dismissed Miss Ginny so he could speak with his son. "Look, Tony, I hear you've been seen with a young woman from the Donato family."

Tony glared at his dad. "I thought that was Ross and Max following us."

"And why wouldn't I have them follow you? I have reasons for keeping our distance from that family."

"I'm twenty-five years old and don't need a babysitter anymore. I have a life outside of your business, Dad, and one that is personal, if you don't mind," Tony said.

Ralph turned and put his hand on Tony's shoulder, "Look, son, your personal life *is* my business, and who you date could mean a matter of life and death to our family."

Tony knew his dad had been into some deep criminal activity, but there were certain secrets that his father kept from him. He shook his head, trying to grasp what his father had just said, but he had a mind of his own. He had to voice his opinion. "I just met this girl, and I'm attracted to her, so if I choose to do so, I will continue to see her."

"And if you care so much for this young lady, then you will let her be."

"What exactly do you have against this family?" Tony asked, shifting his chair closer to the table.

"You know, we deal with certain families, and we have our dealings in this town. Her family, on her mother's side — the Russos — belongs to a clan we have had serious trouble with in the past. Things I'm not willing to discuss with you."

"I've been working for you for five years. I've figured out some things about our family by now. But that was the past. This is now," Tony said, trying to argue his case.

"Family ties still are binding, my son. I'd think you might change your mind if you knew what happened seven years ago in the Benzetti skirmish up in Cleveland."

Tony shook his head and took a deep breath. "Not sure I want to know. I plan on seeing Elena Donato again, and should you choose to have your goonies follow us, so be it."

"I guess that's how it will play out, Tony. But, be warned, her family will most likely have you trailed as well. It's for your date's safety."

That said, Ralph handed Tony his schedule for the day. Tony would head over to Rock Solid, a jewelry store on Market Street, where they had an office in back. He would handle some transactions, most likely involving money from illegal betting and other crimes, with the owners of the mob-run establishment, John Carino and Max Tussi. Tony knew the kind of business he would be taking care of was peanuts compared to what his dad was most likely going to be dealing with in Cleveland that day.

He shook his dad's hand firmly and headed out the door. As he walked out to the driveway, his dad's driver, Ross Vincenzi, pulled up. He waved, and Ross waved back. Ross had been with the family since Tony was a child. A bachelor all his life with no children, Ross was considered family. He was older now; his once dark brown hair and mustache were peppered with silver. Ross had driven him to school every day and picked him up, as his father was always away on business.

As Tony drove to town, he thought about his childhood and his mother, Louisa, whom he missed every day since she passed ten years ago due to cancer. She was the one who had kept their family normal, as normal as they could be. His father never got over her — never remarrying or pursuing any female relationships, as far as Tony was aware. His mother had been a stunning woman with long raven hair and sparkling, emerald-green eyes. She took great pride in her looks, always dressing in the latest fashions. Her illness had struck suddenly after a doctor had misdiagnosed her with digestive problems when, in fact, she had stomach cancer. She declined rapidly over the course of six months.

After grabbing a coffee and a cream roll at a coffee shop, Tony headed over to Rock Solid. Before leaving the car, he looked in his rearview mirror to make sure his covers were outside. He always commanded attention as he entered, dressed as if he were on his way to a formal event. Today was no different. His Italian silk suit had drawn glances from the two clerks who were showing rings to customers. Both ladies smiled and trailed him with their eyes as he sauntered into the back room carrying a black briefcase.

Tony hoped to make a quick business transaction, then find some time to phone Elena and set up another date. She was all he wanted to think about after their last date, but he couldn't think of her now, not here, or he'd get a good hard-on. For now, he had to be on his toes, as he was dealing with John Carino today and exchanging documents and high-end jewelry that had been recovered during a robbery a month ago.

After quickly concluding his business, Tony lit a cigarette and headed out to the parking lot with John in the lead just to make sure all was clear.

John was a large man in his mid-thirties but bore the face of a forty-year-old due to years of stress. There was no room for slip-ups here. It was rumored by one of their informants that the FBI was suspicious of the store's connection to the Marinetti family.

Tony's next stop was The Steel Edge. It was just approaching noon, and since there was no one in the back office, he took the opportunity to phone Elena. He'd hoped she'd answer — he had no idea of what her Monday schedule was like, but it was worth a try. Luckily, she picked up on the second ring.

"I thought maybe you'd be in class," Tony said.

"No, I had two early classes this morning," Elena said, her heart racing in anticipation of an invitation for another date.

They exchanged pleasantries before Tony confessed that she was all he could think about, which made her even more nervous.

He asked her out that Saturday, dinner and a show, her choice for both. He wasn't a moviegoer himself.

Elena agreed, and Tony said he'd call in a few days to see what she'd decided and make reservations at the restaurant of her choice. He added he wanted her to look sexy again for him.

As soon as she ended the call, she threw herself onto her bed, breathless at the thought of another night with this hot hunk. But those thoughts were soon squelched by the thought of breaking the news to her mother. Elena knew her mom would also be breathless, but in a different way.

* * *

After Tony left the house, Ralph phoned John Carino. "We finally have our chance to show the Russo family who rules this town."

"What do you mean? What's going on? Tony just left here."

"My son is dating Lamberto's cousin's daughter, Elena Donato. You know her mother is a Russo — Francesca Russo. All this time, I've been waiting to get revenge on that family," Ralph said firmly.

"You talking about the night of that skirmish in Cleveland, when they shot your cousin Giovanni?" John asked.

"Yes. I am finally going to get justice for him. I know who shot him. The time has come."

"Exactly what did you have in mind?"

"You and Ross Vincenzi will do away with this Elena Donato girl."

There was silence on the other end of the phone. "John … you still there?"

"Yes, I was just thinking about that night and what went down," John said.

"You should know, you were there. Now I'm counting on you."

"You got it, boss. Just let me know how and when."

"Let me get with Ross and coordinate things, and I'll get back to you. And one last thing, we need to keep things under wraps — none of this can make Tony suspicious. He loves this girl. We can't afford to fuck things up."

After ending the call, Ralph's mind wandered back to the night his cousin was shot over a deal gone wrong, gone wrong because of an informant who was a member of the Russo family clan. It was supposed to be a clean robbery, but somehow, they got wind of the huge diamond heist that night and the meeting in Bartlow's Auto Repair garage in Cleveland. Lamberto had waited for Giovanni to leave out the back door with the bag, but he never made it back here.

Ralph stood gazing out of his office window. *It won't be long now until the Russo family feels the pain I did seven years ago.*

Chapter 5

Elena spent the rest of her week on school assignments. Spending time at the Hershel Art Museum on Thursday took up most of her day; she was an art major, and the museum visit was required for one of her classes. Now it was Friday, and that meant she had only one day left to tell her mother she was going on another date with Tony. She'd put it off so long because she didn't want to hear another lecture about the ramifications of dating a mobster.

On her way home after class, she stopped at Navarro's Deli to grab a sandwich to go for lunch. The small deli was packed, and the lines were long, but she was starving and needed food for her drive home.

When she approached the counter, she already knew what she wanted. She ordered an Italian sub and an iced tea. She waited for her order in a booth near the window, looking out on the street. Her eyes were drawn to a silver Lincoln Town Car with two men. Their big hats covered most of their faces. *These can't be the same men who followed Tony and me the other night. That car was black. Wait — could it be Lamberto? But I believe he has a silver Cutlass Supreme. Mom wouldn't do this to me! I mean, I'm not even with Tony.*

Elena was in such a state that she didn't hear her name called from the lunch counter. A man tapped her on the shoulder and asked if she was Elena. She jumped out of her seat and turned around to thank him.

She was out the door with her white paper bag and to-go cup in a flash. She was glad she'd parked in the back lot; the men in the Town Car wouldn't see her leaving. She pulled out onto Market Street, checking her rearview mirror to make sure those men weren't following her.

"You Should Be Dancing" came on the radio, and normally she would be singing out loud, but her mouth was so dry it felt like it was filled with cotton balls. With shaky hands, she reached for the tea in the cup holder and took a sip. Her heart stopped racing as soon as she was close to home. Her mom was still at work, so she had some time to eat lunch and come up with clever ways to tell her about her date tomorrow.

After eating her sandwich, Elena was about to call Pam for some much-needed support, but remembered Pam had classes until late afternoon. Elena headed upstairs to rummage through her closet for an outfit for the date. She remembered what Tony said about looking sexy. She pulled out two minidresses and threw them on the bed. Both were revealing and would satisfy Tony, but she opted for the hot pink one with the plunging neckline. Opening her undies drawer, she realized her options were limited when it came to sexy lingerie. Her black satin bra and panties had seen better days. *I need something to match my dress*, she thought, stuffing the black bra and panties back in her drawer. *I'll have some time tomorrow to run over to that new lingerie shop at South Park Mall.*

Thoughts of wearing sexy new lingerie and pleasing Tony stirred thoughts of pleasing herself as well. She turned on the radio, laid down on the bed, and reached for the small vibrator in her nightstand, sending herself into a frenzy and coming with thoughts of Tony doing naughty things to her.

She heard the garage door open and knew her mom was home from work. She threw on a robe and headed downstairs to face the fire, greeting her mother at the door. "Hey, how was the boutique?"

"Same old thing. The same bored housewives with nothing to do but try on bundles of clothes and walk out with nothing," Fran said as she tossed her keys and purse in the large bowl on the entryway table.

"So ... I thought I'd help with dinner tonight," Elena chirped, her hands on her hips. "What have you got planned?"

"Well, it's Friday night, so why don't we all go to the Railway restaurant for our usual fish fry? I'm sure your father will enjoy that."

"Sounds like a plan."

"Seems like you're in a good mood. Classes okay today?" Fran inquired, opening the refrigerator door to grab a soda.

"Yes, just one class. It was cake."

A brilliant idea just popped into Elena's head. *If I break the news about the date in a public place, then Mom won't make a scene. This is perfect! I'll wait until we have finished our dinner, then break the news; otherwise, she may lose her appetite and have a blowup right there.*

With her new plan in mind, Elena headed to the shower and got dressed. At 5 p.m., her dad arrived home and, since they were starving, they immediately headed out for dinner. They all ordered the Friday fish fry special. As they waited for their food to arrive, Salvatore asked about Fran's and Elena's day.

When the waitress served three steaming plates of fried fish, fries, and coleslaw, Elena's parents dug right in, but Elena ate slowly, feeling butterflies in her stomach. Her mother noticed her picking at her food. "Something wrong with your dinner?"

"Ugh … no … I wanted to discuss something with you," she said, laying her fork down.

Fran held her daughter's gaze. "Oh, no! Please don't tell me this is about that mobster!"

"Now hold on, Fran," Salvatore said, tapping his wife's shoulder. "Calm down. You don't want to make a scene. "

"I can't calm down! Our daughter is making some very bad decisions." Fran slammed her fork on the table, drawing attention from the table next to theirs.

"Mom, I wanted you to know. It's not like I'm sneaking out. And you have no proof that Tony's in the mob.'"

The waitress appeared at the table to see if everything was alright. Salvatore informed her that all was fine and reminded his wife again about making a scene.

"Look, Mom, I'm going out with Tony whether you approve or not. I like him a lot, and he likes me. I'm twenty-two now and can make my own decisions. I don't need your approval."

Fran shot back, "Not when those decisions can bring harm to your family!"

Elena stood up, pushed her chair in, and stormed out of the restaurant. She headed out to the parking lot and leaned up against her parents' Buick LeSabre, pulling her jean jacket tighter around her. The night air had turned quite chilly. She was too mad for tears. Salvatore and Fran were not far behind, meeting Elena by the car.

Silence filled the car on the short ride home until Fran broke the ice. "I can't allow that gangster to come to the house. It's too risky. He'll have to pick you up at Pam's."

Salvatore took his eyes off the road for a second, responding to his wife's demands. "Now you're being totally —"

Elena shot back, "If you say it's too risky for us, then why would you want to implicate Pam and her family?"

"I don't need to explain this to you right now," Fran said, raising her hands in the air.

Elena retreated to her room shortly after they got home and waited for Tony's call, and the fact that she had to tell him he was not permitted at the house had her nerves on edge. It was not going to settle well with him, nor did it settle well with her.

Chapter 6

Elena sat on her bed, holding back tears. Every ten minutes, she glanced at the clock on her nightstand, praying for Tony to call. *Mom is acting like a lunatic. She's batshit crazy!* She had to call Pam before Tony called and make sure it was okay for him to pick her up at her house.

Luckily, Pam answered on the second ring. Elena made her request quickly, not wanting to tie up the phone in case Tony was trying to call. Pam was more than happy to accommodate her request. "Look, I don't even need to tell my folks about this arrangement. Besides, my family has never had any ties to the mob, at least none that I'm aware of."

Elena went silent, thinking about what her friend just said and wishing she were that lucky.

"You still there?" Pam asked. "Listen, I didn't mean anything by that."

"It's okay. I did tell you about my mom's family a while back. I don't keep secrets from my friends."

Elena thanked her friend for being there for her and promised to call her back after Tony called, if he ever did.

Tony's call came shortly after she had hung up with Pam. She made sure to grab it on the first ring before her mother had a chance to answer it on the phone in the kitchen and most likely listen to their conversation.

That deep, sexy voice echoed through the phone, sending chills up Elena's spine. "Are we still on for Saturday night?"

"Y ... yes, but —"

"Everything okay?"

Elena took a deep breath and informed Tony of the ridiculous ban from her house in the most subtle way she could. She apologized profusely to him.

"I get it, babe. Don't worry. All that matters is that I'm with you," Tony said. "And did you pick out a restaurant and movie?"

"I thought we'd go to Top Prime, if that's okay. I hear they have the best prime rib in town."

"Perfect. I'll make our dinner reservations. What about a movie?"

"Haven't looked in the paper yet, but will do tomorrow."

"Or we can discuss it over dinner; there's no rush. I'll pick you up at Pam's on Saturday at 7 p.m. I guess I'll be needing her address."

Elena's heart raced at the thought of seeing him again. She made a quick call to Pam to let her know what time Tony would be there.

"I owe ya, Pam ... I mean ..."

"You only owe me the juicy details on Sunday."

The week flew by. Elena's art assignments for school kept her busy *and* kept her mind off the recent blow-ups with her mother. Her mother had backed off a bit, and she had wondered if her father had laid the law down with her mother. But that was highly unlikely; her mother had always been the boss at home. The only question her mom had asked was where they were going. Of course, Elena told her the truth, then had second thoughts — her mother's cousin and his henchmen might follow her again.

Elena had made a hair appointment on Saturday afternoon and decided to get an updo for a change. She wondered if Tony would like it — she knew how much he liked running his hands through her long, flowing locks.

After putting on the pink minidress, she did her makeup, choosing a bright pink lipstick that complemented her dress. Her new white lace bra and panties would be a welcome treat for Tony if it went that far, as she hoped it would.

Salvatore dropped her off at Pam's at 6:30. He kissed her on the cheek and told her to have a good time. His voice was completely void of any worry.

Pam greeted her at the door and admired her stunning outfit. "Wow! You look hot!"

"Thanks. I hope Tony thinks so, too."

The girls sat on the plush sofa in the living room, gazing out the bay window for the arrival of Tony's red Mustang.

The roar of a car engine had Elena's heart pounding before she saw Tony's car pull into the driveway. She turned to Pam and, with a quick peck on the cheek, said, "Wish me luck."

Tony stood outside the car on the passenger side, waiting to open the door for Elena. "You look stunning, babe!"

"You don't look too bad yourself," Elena said, pulling her dress down a bit as she scooted into the deep leather bucket seat. She loved the way he looked in his black suit jacket and peach colored shirt.

Tony gunned the engine as they headed towards Youngstown Poland Road. When "Don't Go Breaking My Heart" came on the radio, he turned up the volume and shot Elena a meaningful look. Then, out of habit, he glanced in the rearview mirror and saw the black Town Car following him. *Dad's got it covered for tonight,* he said to himself.

The restaurant lot was packed, so Tony opted for valet service. One young man took the keys as another opened the door for Elena.

Tony was quick to appear at Elena's side, grabbing her around the waist, knowing the young valet would most likely be eyeing up his date. Elena liked the fact that Tony was the possessive type. It only turned her on more.

The posh restaurant evoked a classical Greek theme with tall statues of the Greek gods and a lush garden setting. The waiter led them to a private table in the garden room, which held only a few other tables, all of them empty.

"Do you have clout here, too?" she asked as the maître d' pushed in her chair.

Tony flashed her a smile, only to reveal the two deep dimples that made him even more sexy than he already was.

The tall, middle-aged waiter poured sparkling water into the crystal glasses and took their order for drinks.

"May I suggest the calamari Belegria to start?" the waiter asked.

Tony agreed to go with the waiter's suggestion. He reached for Elena's hand. "I can't tell you how sexy you are. I've been thinking about you all week, wondering what you were going to wear."

"Thank you. I'm glad you approve," Elena said, picking up her water to take a sip. Her nerves always gave her a dry mouth.

As the waiter poured wine, Tony lit a cigarette, exhaled, and asked if she had thought about a movie.

In all her nervousness about the date and drama with her mother, that aspect of the date had slipped her mind.

"I … I'm sorry but …"

Just then, the sound of loud gunshots came from the front of the restaurant. Tony quickly stubbed out his cigarette in the ashtray, roughly grabbed Elena's arm, and ducked under the table with her.

"What's happening?!" Elena cried.

Tony went silent, still holding Elena down on the tile floor.

"Tony … Tony? What's going on? Those were gunshots!"

He held her tighter. "Yes, they were. Just stay down here till it stops."

Another waiter entered the room and approached the couple crouched under the table. "Follow me," he said, and swiftly led them down the back hallway to a door.

Elena was pale and shaking. "What's …"

"Don't worry, Miss, we've got you and your date covered."

The waiter spoke directly to Tony. "Your car is here around back; it's safe to leave now." He opened the door and looked out to make sure the Mustang was there.

Tony quickly escorted Elena to the passenger seat, jumped in the driver's seat, and peeled out of the back lot.

As soon as they were on the road, Elena turned to Tony, "Just what the hell was that?"

Tony lit a cigarette before responding. "Let's go somewhere and talk."

Elena was still shaken up but tried to pull herself together. "I guess the movie's out?"

Tony nodded, and Elena could tell from the look on his face that he hadn't appreciated her humor. He seemed worried, too.

The Mustang barreled down Route 422 and pulled into Le Mansion, a five-star hotel on the strip. Tony turned to Elena, "We will talk here. It's okay."

"People don't usually go to a hotel to talk, Tony."

He looked at her and gave her a wink.

Chapter 7

Tony pulled into the circular driveway that led up to the massive hotel entrance. Two valets wearing red vests stood out front. One opened the door for Elena, and she stepped out of the car. Tony was at her side in an instant, having swiftly handed the keys to the young valet.

He placed his hand on the small of her back as he led her to the check-in desk. Elena's eyes scanned the lush décor of the lobby. An impressive floral arrangement sat atop a huge oak pedestal table, its sweet scent permeating the entire lobby. Red velvet couches were positioned strategically around a huge fireplace.

Elena whispered into Tony's ear as he was making arrangements with the front desk clerk. "This place must cost a fortune!"

Tony gave her a quick glance and turned his attention back to the elderly but smartly dressed man awaiting his signature for the reservation.

The man handed Tony a key, and Tony took Elena's hand as they walked toward the elevator. Still within earshot of the front desk, Elena could hear the man at the desk answer a phone call and say the words, "Yes, your son has arrived, and he has a young lady with him."

Elena let go of Tony's hand and turned to him. "So, your father knows we're here? What's going on?"

Tony put his arm around her and told her he'd explain everything once they got to the room.

The elevator doors opened on the fifth floor, and they stepped out onto the plush gold rug in a long hallway. Elena's heart was racing along with her imagination. She needed an explanation, and she needed it now.

The large, luxurious suite was furnished with a king-size bed and had a separate sitting area with a television and a mini kitchenette. There was also a fully stocked bar.

"Exactly how long are we here for?" Elena asked, throwing her purse down onto one of the green velvet chairs.

Tony once again took her hand and led her over to sit on the edge of the bed. "Look, I know I owe you an explanation," he said as he removed his dress jacket, revealing a slender leather holster with a revolver that he removed and set on the oak night table.

"Why in God's name do you have a gun? Who's coming after us?"

Tony's large brown eyes locked with Elena's. "If I tell you the whole truth, I want you to promise you won't run out of here, cuz if you do, it may be dangerous."

"Now you're really scaring me," she said, her voice trembling.

"Those shots tonight — they were friends of my father."

"Some friends! I'd hate to see his enemies!"

"Please, let me finish," Tony insisted. "My father runs a large business faction in this area and in other cities. He has enemies, and, apparently, there were two dangerous men in that restaurant tonight whom he needed to silence."

"And how did you know this? Why would you take me to a dangerous place?"

"I had no idea until I read what the desk clerk had written on the room receipt."

Elena's chest rose and fell as she took a deep breath. "Let me get this right, your father is in the mob, and you are involved as well, and even the desk clerk?"

"No, no. My father knows this is my safe place. He got word of the incident and phoned the hotel. They knew I'd be arriving. The desk clerk is just a desk clerk. I won't lie to you. I'm not in the mob, but if you are referring to my father, then you are correct. I only do some low-profile work for him, you could say."

"Hmm ... low profile, you say." Elena shook her head. "So, I guess you don't have hitman status yet. My mother was right about you. She said to stay clear of you and your family."

"And you ... what do you think?" Tony held her glance, waiting for her reply.

Elena moved in closer to Tony, laying her hand on his chest. "I think it only makes me want you more."

Her words took Tony by surprise. "I thought you were going to walk right out of here once you knew."

"Not a chance in hell." She unbuttoned the first few buttons of his shirt and let her hands roam across his well-sculpted chest. "I like a strong man who leads an active lifestyle."

Tony pulled her head in closer, and their lips met. Her mouth welcomed his tongue, which was eager to explore her warm mouth. His hand pushed her down onto the bed. "I want you to know you are safe with me."

His words only made her hotter, wetter, and wanting more of him.

Her dress was on the floor in minutes, and his pants and boxers were tossed, landing on the bedside table.

He lay beside her, planting little kisses up and down her body, stopping at her folds that were already wet. "You sure you want me?" His voice was soft and sexy.

"More than you know."

Tony got up to reach into his pocket for a condom, as Elena had told him she had been on the pill for two years now.

Tony mounted her and let his fingers slide in and out of her entrance, all the while watching her face to make sure he was pleasuring her. Her moans had confirmed what he wanted to know.

"Fuck me, Tony. Fuck me now!" she pleaded.

"Oh, I love a girl who knows what she wants," he said, using his knees to open her legs wider.

He started with gentle thrusts, which became stronger and longer. They rolled over on the white satin bedspread, facing each other as both were ready to come.

"God, you're beautiful!" Tony said, using his hands to release her long black locks from the structured updo.

And hearing those words, Elena let out a "Yes, now!"

Tony came right with her.

Realizing they hadn't had dinner, Tony ordered sandwiches and a bottle of wine from room service.

After finishing their meal, they lay in bed for the next half hour. Elena had looked at the clock, noting it was well after midnight, and knew she had to call it a night.

They enjoyed a quick shower together in the oversized shower and lathered up with the complimentary strawberry body wash.

Elena dressed as Tony made a call down to the desk to have the valets get the Mustang ready. Elena overheard him mention the names of two men whom she'd assumed were his father's henchmen. She had always been good at eavesdropping to find information. It was how she learned of her mother's family involvement in the mob at a young age. She wondered if Tony knew about their connections. For now, she'd keep it to herself. There was enough new information for one night. She learned so much more about him in the last hour, possibly more than she wanted to know.

Now, she wanted to get to Pam's house. She had mentioned to her mother she'd be spending the night at Pam's and would be home in the morning. The inquisition would have to wait until tomorrow.

Chapter 8

Max Tussi phoned Ralph to let him know his son was safe in the hotel room, as he and Ross Vincenzi had followed the couple since they left the restaurant. They discussed the shooting at the restaurant and how it went down seamlessly. He and Ross were outside in the parking lot, waiting to make sure Ralph's two best hitmen got the job done.

Max inquired about the details for taking care of the Donato girl. Ralph informed him that he, John, and Ross would be getting the details within the next week, and the job would need to be taken care of soon. They'd have to decide which of the two would handle the job. He had devised a plan to take care of the situation without Tony's interference.

Pam jolted awake and jumped from the living room sofa when she heard the roar of Tony's engine pull into the driveway. She had planned to wait up for her friend, making sure she got in safely.

She opened the latch on the front door, expecting Elena to appear within seconds, but peering out the large window, she could see that Elena was still in the car with Tony. She also noticed a black Lincoln Town Car parked two houses down. *Who would be out here so late?* She watched Elena emerge from the Mustang and make a mad dash for the front door.

Elena was breathless as she stepped into the foyer and hugged her friend. "Thank you so much for letting me spend the night."

Pam held her tight, telling her she was always there for her while noticing the pallor of her friend's skin. It was late, and she figured Elena was just tired.

Although it was one o'clock in the morning, Pam was anxious to hear the details of the night. First, Elena peered out the window to make sure Tony had gotten off okay, followed by his dad's bodyguards.

Pam put a hand on Elena's shoulder. "Who's in that Town Car?"

"Long story. It's been quite a night," Elena said, taking off her jacket and sitting down on the sofa.

"Let me make you a hot cup of tea while you go and change in my room. I've got a nightshirt and slippers ready for you, all laid out on the bed."

"You're the best, my dear," Elena replied as she headed off to Pam's room.

Elena welcomed the hot mug of tea as she curled up on the sofa. Pam sat across from her on the overstuffed chair, running her hands through her disheveled hair.

After a couple sips of tea, Elena was ready to spill the highlights of her date. Pam sat on the edge of the chair in anticipation.

My mother was right were the first words that came out of Elena's mouth.

Pam's eyes got as big as saucers. "What? He's in the mob?"

"You could say that. I think his father is a big deal," Elena replied, setting her cup down on a coaster on the coffee table, ready to continue with the details from the night. "There was a shooting at the restaurant tonight. Tony's father's friends shot someone who was a threat to his family."

Pam was silent, trying to comprehend what her friend just said. "Oh, my God! And you want to continue seeing this guy?"

"I'm in love with him. And, besides, he'll keep me protected. I feel safe with him."

"Are you going to tell your mother? I know how she feels about this guy."

"Of course not, unless she finds out."

"You know, word gets around in this town. I'm worried about you, Elena," Pam shook her head.

"You don't have to worry. I'll be just fine."

Elena went on to explain how they escaped the shooting with the help of the waiters at the restaurant.

"So, then where did you go for the next few hours?" Pam asked, her eyebrows knitted together.

"He took me to Le Mansion."

"You mean that huge hotel on Route 422?"

"Yup."

"And you had sex with him after all the commotion?" Pam didn't hold back.

"Yes, and it was the best sex of my entire life!"

Pam sucked in a deep breath, shaking her head. "I just want you to be safe and happy. But you need to be careful, Elena. You know how this town operates. And I know about your mother's family as well."

Elena nodded. "I know I've told you everything. You are my best friend. I trust you. You're the only one I have told this to."

Pam looked at the large brass clock above the brick fireplace. It was 2 a.m. She mentioned that they both needed sleep, especially Elena. Tomorrow morning, she'd drive Elena home. She brought out a large blanket and two pillows and laid them on the sofa, then kissed her friend goodnight and headed toward her room.

Elena snuggled under the blanket, feeling weary from the night's trauma. She was just about to drift off when she heard a sound that seemed to come from the front of the house. She bolted off the sofa and looked out the front window. There was nothing to see. She walked over to the front door and made sure the deadbolt was in place. *Damn, I'm just being paranoid.*

Once back on the sofa, she felt drained from all the commotion that had occurred that night and soon succumbed to a deep sleep.

Chapter 9

Shortly after breakfast, Pam drove Elena home. On the way, Pam reassured her friend she'd always be there for her, no matter what happened with her and her mother.

Elena arrived home just after 9 a.m. She knew her parents would be getting ready for church, so she'd have some time to come up with a sanitized story about her date.

Her mother came downstairs dressed in her Sunday best as Elena had entered the kitchen. "Good to see you home, my dear. How did your evening go?"

Elena could read her mother very well. Her tone was snappy as if she was waiting to hear something she could fire back at her with.

"It was good, I mean ... nothing other than a good dinner," Elena replied, pulling off her jean jacket.

"And did you enjoy the shootout as well?" Fran shot back at her with a sharp tongue.

Elena was frozen. Her mouth opened, forming a perfect O. "How did you ..."

"I think you're smarter than that, my daughter. Did you even realize the danger you'd put yourself in? I don't want to get into this now and get all worked up. Besides, your father and I are late for church, but we will talk when we get back."

"You had your sleazy cousin follow me, didn't you!" Elena's eyes blazed with anger.

Salvatore had come downstairs just in time to interrupt the conversation and gave Elena a firm hug. "Glad you are safe, my dear. I hope you can make it to church with us next Sunday. The coffee's still hot. Have a cup and relax. We'll be back soon."

As soon as her parents shut the door, Elena stormed upstairs to change and call Pam. This was the last straw. She wasn't ten anymore and didn't need her mother's cousin on her tail. Fucking "Lammy." He was bad news, but she suspected there was so much more her mother had not told her.

She phoned Pam before she undressed, needing the support that her friend was more than happy to offer. "Well, I guess your mother has her own resources."

"I don't need this. I mean, if my mother had her cousin follow us, it means she knows about the hotel as well!"

"Now that is creepy!" Pam shot back. "What are you going to do?"

"I'm going to do something. I'll move out if I have to!"

"Now, before doing anything drastic, just calm down. Have a talk with your mom and tell her how you feel," Pam suggested. "You can always spend a few nights here if need be."

"Oh, that will go over well. Ugh, I'm just beyond stressed."

"Well, call me later today and let me know what you have worked out," Pam said.

Elena took a much-needed hot shower. After she had towel-dried, she headed for her room to get dressed. It was a warm day, so she figured a walk in the local park would help clear her head.

Before she had a chance to get dressed, the phone rang. It was Tony making sure she was okay. "I hope you weren't too rattled at what went on last night. I can promise you that was a rarity. It won't happen again."

Elena didn't want to tell him all the sordid details about what went on with her and her mother.

He could tell by the tone of her voice that she was upset and didn't want to push the matter further. He carried on about the sex they had had last night and how he couldn't stop thinking about her. He asked her to dinner next Saturday at his father's home.

"My father would like to meet you. His chef is making a special homemade Italian dinner for us if you say yes."

"I ... I don't know what to say." *He's really upped the ante,* Elena said to herself.

"Say yes!" Tony's voice was authoritative.

"I'm speechless and nervous. I mean, meeting your father! And he has his own chef? Wow!"

"Nothing to worry about. He's as gentle as a lamb. He'll love you."

The word "lamb" brought to mind her mother's cousin, the hit man, but Elena accepted the invitation. Tony said he'd call her during the week to let her know what time he'd pick her up at Pam's house. He knew without Elena saying anything that he would still be banned from her home.

After hanging up with Tony, Elena knew this was getting serious. She sat on her bed, still wrapped in her shower towel. *There's no way I'm telling Mother. I'll be dining at a mobster's house for dinner. God only knows what she'd do.*

She quickly dressed and drove to Mill Creek Park before her folks arrived home. She needed some time to process everything that had happened. She brought her sketchpad and pencils, knowing she had a drawing assignment for her class. A landscape drawing of the park would be perfect.

Elena was glad to find the park empty. She felt like being alone and didn't want to chat with anyone. It was a beautiful state park; almost everyone in the Youngstown area, including tourists, visited frequently. As the morning warmed up, she abandoned her jean jacket and followed the trail that led to the creek.

She sat on the edge of the creek listening to the birds and other sounds of nature. She opened her notebook to start sketching the park — sketching always cleared her head. A red cardinal landed on a bush on her right, almost as if he were some kind of messenger. She had been brought up to believe these birds were messengers from the other side. Maybe it was a messenger from her grandmother Russo, who'd passed just last Christmas. She had been very close to her and spent many hours in her company, listening to her tales of growing up in the old country, back in her village in Italy. Just as she was about to sketch the cardinal, he flew off.

She wondered what her grandmother would think of her dating Tony. After all, it was her mother's side of the family that had Mafia connections in Sicily and here in Ohio. Her mind wandered off, not aware of the time, until a group of people came walking by, chatting about what a wonderful afternoon it was. She looked at her watch, noting it was past noon. She knew she had to return home and have that talk with her mother. She would stand her ground. She loved Tony no matter who he was, a mobster's son or not.

Opening the garage door, she noticed her parents' white Buick was parked inside. As she entered the house, she could smell spaghetti sauce cooking. The spicy aroma wafted through her nostrils, making her tummy rumble.

Her mother was at the stove, stirring a big pot, and turned to welcome her with a hug. "Are you hungry?"

"I'm starving."

"Dinner won't be ready till five, so I'll make some sandwiches for lunch, then we can talk," her mother said, wiping her hands on her flowered apron.

Elena felt the energy had shifted for the better in the house. Her mother seemed calmer, and Elena herself felt better. *Maybe that cardinal was Grandmother sending some good vibes,* she thought as she helped her mother make ham and provolone sandwiches. She didn't want any drama, but she was prepared to state her case.

After lunch, Salvatore told the two of them to go for a walk, and he'd mind the sauce as well as clean up the lunch dishes. When Elena went to give him a peck on the cheek, he winked at her, and she smiled back. *Maybe things were going to turn out for the better*, she hoped. But if things went south, she was ready to deal with that as well.

Her mother had changed into capris and a t-shirt, ready for a stroll around the neighborhood. Elena opted for shorts and a tank top. The afternoon had climbed into the 70s, which was usual for late April.

Fran turned to Elena at the end of the driveway, "Let's head up toward the Dairy Queen at the top of the street. We can have a treat, then walk off our calories on the way back."

Yeah, ice cream always makes it better, at least that's what I thought when I was a child, reflected Elena. *A shot of whiskey is more fitting for this mother-daughter chat.*

Chapter 10

Elena and Fran sat on the picnic tables outside Dairy Queen, waiting for their orders. Fran took a deep breath and let out what she had been holding in since early this morning. "Look, Elena, I know what went on last night. Now I don't want to get into a fight with you. We've already had too many blow-ups over this issue. But I want to be honest with you."

Elena looked at her mom and shook her head. She had no words. She'd listen to what her mother had to say, but nothing could change her mind about her relationship with Tony.

The woman at the serving window called their names. Fran rose, but Elena remained seated on the bench.

"Aren't you coming?" Fran asked.

Elena rose slowly, following her mother as if it were a chore to retrieve her large chocolate cone.

After they returned to the table, Fran revealed some information Elena wasn't prepared to hear. "Lamberto followed you last night. He told me about the shooting and why it happened. He was there to make sure you were safe."

"And how in the hell was he supposed to do that?" Elena asked, after taking a few licks of her cone. "I don't need that pudgy-faced bulldog in my business!"

"You know how. He was armed and had backup. He told me a Pittsburgh faction was after Tony's father's men. But I guess you already know that, if Tony had told you. "

"Yes, mother, I knew that. Tony, being the gentleman he is, came clean and told me everything."

"You will never know everything when you are involved with men like this."

"I guess you'd know. Seems you know everything that's going on in my life these days." Elena's eyes narrowed. She felt as though her body couldn't hold any more anger inside. She swallowed hard before saying something she hoped she wouldn't regret.

"I guess you know I spent the night with him at the hotel."

Her mother shook her head in disapproval.

Elena got up and headed toward the trash bin, having no desire to finish her cone.

"There's something else you need to know — something bad."

Elena stopped and returned to the bench, ready to listen to what her mother had to say.

"Seven years ago, up in Cleveland, there was a skirmish. Lamberto took out Ralph Marinetti's cousin. It was self-defense, so to speak, but the Marinettis didn't see it that way and never will. They've made several attempts at revenge on our family — ones you've never been aware of — all because of Lamberto and his men, who've had our backs."

Elena locked eyes with her mother. "So, what makes you think Tony's family is any worse than ours?"

"We're not in the business of taking over territories like the Marinettis are. We are all in danger. The only ones left in our family that provide protection these days are Lamberto and Dominic Terruza. And as long as you continue this relationship with Tony, Lamberto, and his friend, Dominic, will be involved."

Elena rose and dumped her cone into the trash, turning around to inform her mother she was heading home and not to follow her.

Fran stood yelling back at her daughter, "Elena … please! Listen to me!"

With deaf ears, Elena headed back home. She had a plan and was ready to enact it the minute she got in. She'd call Pam and ask if she could stay a few days with her. She needed to get away, to cool off, but more than that, she needed to let her mother know their relationship was on shaky ground.

Elena flew past her father, who was reading the newspaper on the living room sofa, and bounded up the stairs.

"Where's your mother? What's wrong?" Salvatore dropped the paper to the floor.

No answer came, so he headed up to Elena's room to see what was going on. She was on the phone with Pam and told him she'd explain in a few minutes.

Salvatore heard the door slam, and Fran yelled for him to come downstairs. She informed him that the mother-daughter chat didn't go so well, and he replied that she was indeed pushing their daughter further and further away.

Pam was more than happy to provide her friend with refuge for a few days. Her parents loved Elena since the girls were children.

After she finished her call with Pam, Elena began throwing things into a suitcase. She figured it'd be at least three days, and she'd need some casual clothes for school. She planned to stop at the bank and withdraw some cash for food and gas.

Grabbing her jean jacket, suitcase, and purse, she headed downstairs into the kitchen, where her parents were sitting at the table. "I don't want you to worry. I'm leaving for a few days just to clear my head. I'll be at Pam's."

Salvatore shot out of his seat and hugged her. "I think maybe this is just what you need. Thank you for letting us know. I know you'll be fine there. Call us if you need anything."

Fran continued to sit at the table as Elena headed to the door. She dropped her head in her hands. She had no words; if she said anything, she might regret it.

Elena felt freedom the minute she pulled out of the driveway and hit Youngstown Poland Road on her way to Pam's. She'd call Tony as soon as she arrived.

By the time Elena arrived at Pam's, it was 2 p.m. Pam met her at the door. As soon as Elena set her things down, Pam suggested they head out to Yellow Creek Park, a small park just a few blocks away, for a walk. She knew Elena loved nature and thought it would be the best thing to calm her down. It was another one of her favorite parks where she spent many hours enjoying the landscape and sketching assignments for her art class.

The girls walked along a path until Pam suggested they take a break. They drove to Coffee Corner, where the lot was pretty much empty. That was fortunate, because Pam knew her friend wouldn't want anyone to listen in on their conversation. This town had too many prying eyes and ears. It thrived on gossip.

They sat in a back booth and ordered chocolate shakes. Pam was the first to speak. "I wanted to tell you that my folks are fine with you staying as long as you like. You know how easy they are."

"Well, I wish my mother was that easy. This has gotten ridiculous!"

"I hear you. But she's just trying to protect you," Pam said, pulling out a few napkins from the chrome napkin holder on the table. "Tell me again what exactly happened the other night."

Elena disclosed most of the details of the night, leaving out the more graphic ones regarding the sex.

Pam grabbed her hand from across the table. "I'd be scared out of my mind if that happened! No wonder your mother is worried."

Elena was just about to respond when the shakes arrived. She took a sip of her shake and prepared to say something that would most likely shock her friend. "To tell you the truth, I thought it was hot!"

Pam looked up at her friend quizzically. "You gotta be kidding me!"

"Nope. It only makes him hotter. It's like I'm in some kind of James Bond movie." Elena's cheeks turned red.

"Let me tell you, girl, this is not some movie; this is the real deal. I hope you know what you're dealing with."

"Oh, I do. Trust me, Mother!"

"I'm not your mother, but I do worry about you. I want you to be happy. Just be safe, and if that means putting up with your mom's cousin following you around, so be it. Maybe it's a good thing?"

The girls finished their shakes and headed out to the parking lot.

As they walked to the car, they noticed a newer black Town Car parked at the far end of the lot, its windows tinted so dark they couldn't see who was inside.

"Get in!" Elena shouted to Pam, who quickly unlocked the car.

Chapter 11

Ralph Marinetti had organized a meeting with Ross Vincenzi and Max Tussi at his satellite office in Cleveland. John Carino was minding Rock Solid, the jewelry store, and would be filled in with the details later. The meeting was in an older produce warehouse, one Ralph owned or had taken over and used as a cover for his secret business deals. The two men sat across from Ralph at his desk, eager to hear the plans for kidnapping the Donato girl.

Ross removed his hat, revealing a severely receding hairline. He was no spring chicken anymore. He would be turning sixty-two next month and had been more than just a driver and protector for the family; he had done many favors for Ralph over the years, many of which could not be classified as driving duties. Max, on the other hand, was in his mid-forties and had the body of a bouncer, having worked out regularly at the local gym for years. He had joined the gym after a member of his family had a run-in with Lamberto a few years back and was eager for revenge.

"Okay, gentleman, we know Elena has morning classes at Youngstown State. You've followed her there. It's too bad she doesn't have a night class. But we can't let broad daylight affect our plan," Ralph said, smoothing his thinning black hair back behind his ears.

"We know she parks in the south parking deck. It's older and not well-lit. Most students don't park there; they use the new deck on the north end," Max said.

"We need to find out what time she comes back to her car after class. And from what I know, the times sometimes change," Ralph said. "She may not have classes every day."

"So, I guess that means we find out what time her first class is, follow her and sit in the car waiting," Ross said, fiddling with his hat in his lap.

"That's the plan. I'll try to get the lowdown on her schedule from Tony. In fact, I have invited the Donato girl for dinner this weekend to my house. I can casually act like I'm interested and ask her."

"Great plan, boss. Tony will be pleased you are interested in his girl-friend," Max said, nodding his head.

"Yes, and when she's disappeared, Tony, thinking that I like the girl, will have no reason to suspect me. She's not like the usual putannas Tony has dated in the past."

"You know, Ralph, for a man who never went to college, you're pretty smart," Max replied.

"Yeah, all that book learning don't mean shit when you have all the experience I have." Ralph's grin made his sagging jowls more pronounced.

Ralph poured the men a shot of bourbon as he went over the details for the kidnapping. "You'll inject her with a dose of Midazolam that I received from a doctor friend. I got two vials. One should be plenty for this young gal. The second one is just insurance. It will take effect in seconds. Once she's out, carry her to the car and drive to Lake Erie. Tie her up with rope attached to a few cement blocks and dispose of her body in the lake. You boys know the ropes, excuse the pun," Ralph added.

"Lake Erie must be getting kinda full," Max joked.

Ignoring Max's joke, Ralph continued, "So, you boys can start to scope her out this week. Keep me posted. We all know that every detail is important. There can be no slip-ups. I'll be filling John in later. And always assume someone from the Russo family might be trailing you."

"Oh, you mean like that geriatric Lamberto?" Ross asked.

"Never know, but I think I've heard from some of the guys in Youngstown that he is out of the loop," Ralph added, setting his empty tumbler down on the desk.

"When one leaves, there's always someone else to take their place," Max said.

Ralph sighed, "We'll go ahead with our plan, boys, and last, but not least, I want to remind you to pick up your new toys, the Smith and Wesson .357 Mags and your Colt 1903 Hammerless, over at Dawson's garage tomorrow night. Old man Reno will be expecting you."

Max and Ross exited the building after the lookout signaled all was clear.

The two men were glad to get back on their familiar turf in Youngstown before having to spend a few days on their new mission. Being in this business, one never knew if they'd see their family members and friends again. They had both had too many close calls over the past few years.

Chapter 12

A week passed, and Elena was still camping out at Pam's house. Ruth, Pam's mother, was more than happy to have Elena but was beginning to wonder how long her stay would last. She had a chat with her daughter while Elena was at school.

"You know, Pam, I love Elena like a second daughter and don't want her to feel as though we're kicking her out, but at some point, she'll have to go back home. I've had several calls from her mother. I reassured her that Elena is all right. I know how concerned I would be."

"Thanks, Mom. I know you're aware of her situation and understand. I believe she is seeing Tony this Saturday and said she will most likely return home this Sunday."

Ruth sighed, "You know, I pray Tony isn't the bad guy her mother makes him out to be. I'd hate to see her get involved with a crime family."

Pam went silent, searching for words. She never told her mother about the shooting at the restaurant that night, but wondered if Fran had.

Pam reassured her mother that she had met Tony and he was a cool guy. She had to convince her mother of that, or she would not want her involved in this kind of thing. "He treats Elena like a queen, and I believe they're in love. I know he'd never allow Elena to be in danger."

Ruth went about preparing dinner while Pam retreated to her room to work on a class assignment. She thought about how they had been followed at lunch the other day and worried these men were still out there following her friend.

When Friday rolled around, Elena was in a panic, wondering what to wear to Tony's house for dinner. She talked Pam into going to South Park Mall with her to find the perfect dress, classy and not too sexy. She wanted to make a good impression on his father, mobster or not.

While scouring the racks of dresses at Style Haven, Pam pulled out a couple of black knee-length cocktail dresses.

Elena gave her a serious look, "It's not a funeral for God's sake!"

"No, but black is classic, and these are simple," Pam replied. "His father is most likely old-school Italian."

Elena nodded and grabbed the dresses, and they both headed to the fitting rooms. The second dress was a hit. Elena had to admit her friend was right. She twirled around in the mirror, admiring the way it hugged her curves.

Pam initiated a heart-to-heart chat on the way home about Elena's long-term plans when her friend dropped a bombshell on her.

"Well, when I talked to Tony last night, he mentioned that I may never have to go home again. He had a plan and said it was a surprise and he'd tell me at dinner tomorrow night. So, plan on your roommate departing on Sunday morning."

Pam took her eyes off the road for a minute. "What is that supposed to mean?"

"Not sure, but if my dreams come true, he'll ask me to move in with him."

"But he lives at home with his father."

"No, I believe we'll get an apartment or something. I can just feel it!" Elena bubbled with excitement.

"Oh, I'm sure that'll go over well with your mother."

"I'm not worried about that now. I'm thinking of my future with Tony."

Pam nodded, wondering what that would actually look like.

Tony was busy himself that Saturday morning, helping his father make arrangements for the dinner. His father chose takeout from Rossini's over his personal chef for the evening, scheduling delivery for 6 p.m. Tony would pick up Elena at 5:30.

After running a few errands for his father, Tony headed over to the Rock Solid jewelry store. This time it was not a business trip; he wanted to buy a gold bracelet for Elena. He wanted to give her something special, something that would make her want to move in with him.

One of the salesladies motioned him over and whispered in his ear that John Carino was waiting for him in the back. John, a middle-aged, attractive man dressed in an Italian silk suit, led him to a long table displaying an impressive selection of stunning gold bracelets ranging from Cartier to Tiffany & Co.

Tony's eyes lit up as he viewed each bracelet in its original black velvet case. John informed him that he had his pick, "on the house." Tony knew exactly what that meant. He knew how these luxurious pieces were acquired, but he was overcome with anticipation of choosing the one that would please Elena.

He selected the classic Cartier 18k gold LOVE bracelet. It was simple, yet elegant, with an engraved letter L on the outside.

John had told him the L represented Love. Tony liked that. He also got the nerve to ask what the bracelet was worth. He wished he hadn't after John revealed the price was a hefty $6,000. He sucked in a deep breath and knew it was perfect for Elena.

John had offered to wrap it up for him. "She must be one special lady."

Tony flashed a smile. "She sure is."

As soon as Tony left, John thought about Elena Donato and how her life was soon coming to an end. *Shame, the boy really seems to love her.* He shook his head and began putting away the many pieces he had laid out on display.

Chapter 13

Elena was about to hang up the phone with her mother, after informing her she'd most likely be home this coming Sunday, but that it may be temporary if things worked out the way she'd hoped. Fran was quick to ask her daughter exactly what that meant, and Elena didn't hold back her words — she never did. "I really think Tony is going to ask me to move in with him."

Silence on the other end of the phone. Elena didn't hear a click, so she knew her mother was still on the line. "Mom ... Mom, you still there?!"

"I ... I'm here, Elena. Just taking it all in. You mean you'd live in his father's house? That mobster's home!"

"No, we'd get our own place, maybe an apartment. The last time I saw him, he talked about how wonderful it would be if that could happen."

"My darling daughter, I thought by now you'd realize the ramifications of your decisions, but I see you have gotten deeper into something you will eventually learn to regret."

"Look, Ma, I don't want an argument. I'm too excited to finally get to meet Tony's dad and have a special dinner at his house."

Salvatore had just entered the kitchen and grabbed the phone from his wife. "I'm looking forward to seeing you. Maybe we can spend Sunday as a family by going out to dinner or whatever you like."

Fran just stood there, her eyebrows knitted together, shaking her head. When the phone call ended, she was quick to let her husband know her feelings. "This is worse than I thought! She's dining at that mobster's home tonight and may end up moving in with Tony!"

Salvatore grabbed his wife and held her tight, trying to calm her down as best he could, but there was no point in trying when she was this worked up. He feared the worst, knowing her history of what had occurred with her family in the past.

Fran waited until Salvatore had gone to the store to call Lamberto. As soon as she heard the garage door close, she was dialing his number, the secret one only she was privy to. *It was time to put an end to this so-called romance. Salvatore doesn't have to know. It's best this way, for if he did, he might interfere with my plans.*

Fran caught Lamberto just as he was leaving the house. He agreed to stop by her house that evening to discuss her plan. That night, Salvatore would be out, meeting a few friends at the Italian Club to play bocce.

Lamberto was eager to hear her plan. He had a bad feeling about Elena moving in with Tony and would protect her at all costs.

Fran felt a migraine coming and rubbed her temples, but it didn't stop her from baking the homemade biscotti cookies her cousin loved. The best laid plans were always accompanied by good, strong coffee and homemade cookies. She told Salvatore she was in the mood for the biscotti – he had no idea Lamberto would be visiting.

Fran decided that they'd sit outside on the back patio since the night was warm. She cleaned the outdoor furniture in anticipation of her cousin's arrival. She didn't have to worry about her nosey elderly neighbor lady — she was gone for a few weeks on a visit to her son in Columbus. The other neighbor, to the right of her, was always at the church for bingo on Saturday nights.

Seeing the silver Cutlass Supreme pull into the driveway made Fran's heart race. She had counted on her cousin to do what she couldn't — just as he always did.

Lamberto listened intently as his cousin laid out exactly what she wanted him to do to Tony. He was to work him over, so he was injured but not dead.

"Let me get this right, you're telling me to go gentle on the kid?"

"I want him to get the message, if you know what I mean," Fran said, pouring Lamberto a cup of coffee.

"It will be like taking candy from a kid," Lamberto smiled, shaking his head. "Your wish is my command. I don't want our Elena falling into the hands of that family either."

Lamberto's words helped settle Fran's nerves, and she hoped this little attack would put an end to this relationship for good.

"You know, she's going to put two and two together and realize who did this. She's smart."

"I don't care. I'd rather have a live, smart daughter than a dead one. She's so blindly in love she doesn't see what she's getting into."

Lamberto finished his coffee and grabbed another cookie to go. He had to get home and call his friend Dominic Teruzza; he might need backup. Dominic, or Dom as he was called, had been his friend since childhood. They were always there to help each other out when needed. Dom was a large man with broad shoulders and built like a battleship. People moved out of the way to avoid him.

Popping the shiny box with the glittery bow in the glove box, Tony headed home to see if his dad needed help for this evening. He planned to give Elena the bracelet after dinner when he asked her to move in with him. He hoped her answer would be yes, especially after all the trouble she was going through with her mother.

Elena was beyond excited as she slipped into the black cocktail dress. Pam had agreed to help her with her makeup and hair. Both girls sat at the vanity in Pam's room, chatting about what the night might look like.

"I'm so nervous about meeting his father," Elena said as she opened a palette of silver eyeshadows. "I hope those things my mother said about him aren't true. I mean, what happened at the restaurant the other night doesn't mean he's a hardcore killer."

"Even if he is, would you still continue to see Tony?"

"Of course, I would. I'm in love with him. He's not the same person his father is," Elena said, watching Pam pile her hair up into a topknot, then adding a rhinestone barrette.

"Ya think I look a bit overdone?"

"You can never look overdone when you're about to meet your possible father-in-law."

"What?" Elena whipped her head around so fast she could have gotten whiplash. "Are you kidding me ... father-in-law?"

"You never know," Pam said, reaching for a huge can of hairspray to make sure her 'do stayed in place.

"Well, I can tell you one thing: if we ever did get married, my mother would have a heart attack! We'd most likely have to run off to get married. Vegas, maybe."

Pam nodded. "Make sure to invite me. I've never been there."

It was almost time for Tony to arrive. Elena took one last look in the full-length mirror. Pam clapped her hands and said she looked like Audrey Hepburn.

Lamberto was about to leave the house when Fran called. He wasn't expecting to hear from her because she had gone over all the details regarding Tony the other night. But his cousin was prattling on, reiterating everything they'd discussed before.

"Yes, make sure he's not hurt too badly, just rough him up enough so he gets the message. He'll figure this out soon enough. And make sure you wait until he drops Elena off at Pam's house. I don't want Elena to see any of this."

"I get it, cuz. No worries. I got Dom with me, too."

"Good idea because I'm sure Marinetti has his henchmen following those kids tonight," Fran said.

"I'm not worried about them. Dom and I have plans in case they try to interfere," Lamberto replied in a reassuring tone. "Now don't you worry. I'll call you as soon as I get home. This is a piece of cake for me. You know that."

"Do I ever. Just make sure our Elena is safe."

"You have my word."

Lamberto pulled on his suit jacket with his holster securely in place and headed into the garage. He was eager to try out his new toy if need be. He knew Dom would be carrying as well. This was supposed to be an easy trailing, but he knew from past experiences that shit happens. He picked up a few snacks at the Italian market on the way to picking up Dom. Then, they headed into Youngstown to Wick Avenue, where they would sit a few blocks down from Ralph Marinetti's mansion. It was going to be a long night.

Chapter 14

Elena kept looking at the large brass sunburst clock above the fireplace. She was counting down the minutes until Tony arrived.

Pam kept reassuring her that she looked stunning. She took hold of her friend's hand, and it was shaking. "Look, there's nothing to be nervous about. Your mom's cousin is following you, and Tony's dad has his men in tow as well. I don't think the Queen of England has that much security."

"Well, that part makes me wonder how close they are looking. And even if those rumors about his dad are true, how do I know he'll want Tony to be involved with a commoner, I mean, the family's got money — lots of it."

"You're not some low-life vagrant he picked up off the street, Elena. I'm sure his dad will be glad Tony's found a decent, respectable girl," Pam said as she tucked a stray hair back up into Elena's updo.

The girls jumped when they heard the roar of the Mustang's high-powered engine in the driveway. Pam's mother popped into the living room to wish Elena good luck and remind her that she's there for her if anything seems off.

Elena turned to her with a worrisome look, wondering if Pam's mother believed what her mother had told her.

"All will be fine, dear, enjoy yourself," Ruth said.

Pam and her mother walked into the kitchen to give Elena privacy. Elena opened the door to find Tony decked out in jeans and a mint-colored polo, minus his signature black leather jacket, as it was a warm night.

Tony hugged her and whispered into her ear, "You look so damn hot, I think we'll just skip dinner and head to a motel."

Elena blushed as she closed the door behind her. Tony opened the passenger side door for her, but she stopped to glance around, searching for the black Town Car. It was nowhere in sight, and neither was Lamberto's silver Cutlass. *Hmm, maybe everyone has realized they don't need to be on my tail every time I'm with Tony*, she breathed a sigh of relief.

As they rode down Wick Avenue, Elena's eyes scanned the huge mansions and the lush landscaping that adorned each property. Her pulse quickened as they turned onto Walnut Drive. Tony stopped the car at a huge black iron gate with a small guardhouse, minus a guard, and rolled his window down to push a few buttons. The gates opened, revealing a long driveway that led up to an enormous brick mansion with white pillars. He took her hand and squeezed it, knowing she was nervous.

He parked the car in the circular driveway, where Ross was waiting, wearing his chauffeur outfit. He came around to greet Tony. "I'll park the car in the back garage," he said.

Tony introduced Elena to Ross. "This man is like a second father to me," he said. "I don't know what I'd do without him. He's had my back too many times."

Elena shook Ross's hand as he told her to enjoy dinner. He told Tony he was a lucky man to have such a lovely lady to join him.

Just then, a strong breeze came out of nowhere, causing water from a large fountain close to the driveway to spray onto Elena's dress. "Oh, great! Just what I need!"

"It only makes you look sexier," Tony said.

"Sexy is not what I'm going for tonight!"

A middle-aged butler greeted them at the door. Tony introduced Elena to Martin, whose haunting looks reminded her of Lurch from "The Addams Family."

Elena's eyes took in the massive winding staircase with a shiny oak banister, assuming a maid must have polished it for hours. They followed Martin into a large dining area that was decorated as though there was to be a formal gala. An ornate crystal chandelier hung over a long oak table that was covered with a white lace tablecloth. Six high-back white velvet chairs graced either side of the table. There were three place settings on the table. Elena could tell the china was of good quality, and she admired the real crystal goblets sparkling in light reflected from the chandelier.

As Elena took in the fine artwork that adorned the walls, one in particular caught her eye. It was one of a beautiful dark-haired woman with an olive complexion wearing a red satin dress. She turned to Tony, "I guess this would be your mother?"

"Yes, it is."

"She's absolutely beautiful!"

"She certainly was!" came a strong, raspy voice from behind Tony. She turned to see a short, pudgy man. She knew right away it had to be Ralph.

Ralph offered his hand to Elena. "Nice to meet you. I'm Tony's father."

"It's a pleasure, sir. Thank you for inviting me to your lovely home."

Ralph pulled out a chair and gestured for Elena to sit. Tony sat next to her, and Ralph sat across from them.

Martin had entered the room and filled their goblets with sparkling water, as another young waiter who worked for the restaurant Ralph had hired passed a tray of toasted bruschettas. Elena reached for one and set it onto her appetizer plate. *I'd better not spill anything on these white velvet chairs, she thought; they must have cost a fortune.*

"So, I've heard some good things about you," Ralph said, reaching for a bruschetta. "Tony says you're a college girl."

Elena blushed. She filled Ralph in on her studies, attempting to make simple conversation. Her nerves hadn't quite settled down yet, but when she saw the waiter come in holding a bottle of wine, she knew help was on the way.

"I hope you like veal scallopine," Ralph said.

"Oh, I love it. My grandmother used to make it."

"Tony tells me you're also Italian."

Hearing those words, Elena just about choked on her water.

"You okay?" Tony asked as he patted her on the back.

"Yes ... yes, I'm fine. And yes, to answer your question. My parents are both full-blooded Italians. My mother's mother was born in Sicily. The Russo family name is known throughout the area. Not sure if you've heard of it."

"In fact, I have," Ralph said, nodding his head. "Good lineage, I'll say."

"Dad's parents hail from Rome.

"See, good blood in that family," Tony added.

"Indeed. And I think we need a toast to that," Ralph said, reaching for his empty glass.

The young waiter poured a deep burgundy wine into each glass as Ralph led the toast. "Here's to good wine and great bloodlines. Salute!"

Ralph didn't want to let on that he'd heard of the Russo family name, nothing to make Elena suspicious.

The conversation was kept quite light, with Tony telling his dad about Elena's art classes at the university and Elena nodding after Tony's compliments. They enjoyed the rest of the meal, and Elena had patted her stomach when Martin came in with a tray of tiramisu. "Oh, I feel as though I couldn't eat another bite, but I won't pass up a small piece of my favorite dessert."

"Your lady has good taste," Ralph said, signaling the waiter to pour him another glass of wine.

Elena blushed with that compliment. Tony, knowing she was uncomfortable during the entire meal, gave Elena's foot a slight tap with his foot under the table. He stood up, addressing his father, "Everything was wonderful tonight, Papa, but I need to get this young lady home."

Martin had come out with a plate wrapped in plastic, which held a huge piece of tiramisu to take home.

"My father is old-school Italian. Guests always leave with some food."

Elena thanked Ralph, and he hugged her. "I'm glad Tony has a good woman, finally."

Tony looked at Elena, who was searching for words. "I ... I don't know what to say."

"Say you'll come back again," Ralph said as he walked them to the door.

Ross had pulled the Mustang around and opened the door for Elena as she took a seat, still holding the dessert plate. He flashed her a wide smile.

He rounded the car to say goodbye to Tony and gave him the sign that he'd be following them as usual.

"She was a hit tonight, Ross. I knew she would be. Dad likes her." Tony was so proud of how things had gone tonight.

Upon hearing the words *hit tonight,* Ross froze. His face had grown pale, causing Tony to notice.

"You okay, Ross?"

"Yeah, just tired, young man. Drive safe now and get that fine lady home."

Tony gave Ross a wink.

Ross sauntered into the triple garage to start the Town Car. He sat there replaying Tony's words. He couldn't get them out of his head. *Hmm, she was a hit, alright, and with Ralph's plans, she'll miss the usual hit but meet her death differently. Tony looked so happy. He's in love. How can I do this to her? To him?*

Ross was unaware of Lamberto and Dominic, who were sitting at the end of the block, also waiting to follow the couple. They planned to wait until Tony dropped Elena off, then follow Tony as he made his way home, tailing him closely so he'd pull off to the side where Lamberto would issue his warning in the physical sense. They had to make sure Ross was out of sight as well.

Ross pulled out soon after Tony left, but slowed down, hearing the car phone ring. It was Ralph. He boasted about how his plan was in the works, and by this time next week, Elena would be long gone, and the Marinetti family would have reason to celebrate.

Chapter 15

As soon as the car rounded the corner, Tony put his hand on Elena's thigh. "I couldn't contain myself in there. You look so fucking hot, Elena. I want to take you back to the hotel and have wild sex with you. My cock is about to burst through my jeans!"

Elena didn't have to think twice about Tony's suggestion. She wanted him just as bad as he wanted her.

The Mustang roared down Route 422 toward Le Mansion. Tony looked in his rearview mirror to see if Ross was following him. He could see the Town Car two cars behind him, while Lamberto and Dominic were just a few cars behind Ross's.

Once again, a valet stood outside the hotel entrance. The young man opened the door for Elena, and Tony was quickly at her side. They headed into the lobby toward the check-in desk.

When Ross noticed Tony's usual maneuver, he decided to take a quick break and head for a bite to eat at the café a few blocks away, then return to sit in the lot of the hotel waiting for Tony's departure. He figured the couple would be there for at least a few hours, knowing how Tony operated. He also knew Tony was serious about Elena.

Lamberto and Dominic pulled in after the valet had taken the Mustang to the back lot. Dominic turned to his boss, "We just gonna sit in this freaking parking lot all night like two chooches? I mean, I ain't even had supper yet!"

"Oh, shut your trap, Dom, I've got some Italian subs in the cooler on the back seat. I came prepared. Besides, you're getting paid pretty damn good."

"And when are we gonna work this hood over?"

"Don't worry. I have instructions from Fran to wait until he drops Elena off at her friend's house. Then we'll cut him off and give him a few punches," Lamberto said as he reached into the back seat to retrieve the cooler.

A much younger dark-haired man was at the front desk. Tony didn't recognize this guy, but he had to be on guard and suspicious of everyone. He couldn't take chances, not while Elena was with him.

Tony told Elena to take a seat on the velvet settee in the center of the lobby while he made arrangements for a room. Elena wondered if Tony had already planned this move or if it was last-minute.

Tony asked the desk clerk to phone his father, and said the bill would be taken care of by his dad. He figured this guy was new because most of the staff knew him and his father, and the usual arrangements they had.

After reaching Ralph, the young man apologized to Tony, then handed him a few papers, along with a key to a luxury suite.

As they waited for the elevator to take them up to the fourth floor, Tony kissed Elena and whispered into her ear, "I can't wait to get you into bed."

This suite was different from the last one they'd been in. It was more opulent with a larger sitting area and a small kitchenette. It had a balcony overlooking the pool area, but the first thing Tony did was close the green velvet drapes. "We don't need any onlookers."

A sudden chill ran up Elena's spine. "Are we expecting anyone?"

"No, babe. But if we do, I've got us covered." Tony removed his jacket and set his Ruger on the oak entry table.

Elena ran her hands up and down his toned arms. "This is what turns me on. A man who's not afraid. A man who's a real man."

Tony was always surprised by Elena's no-fear attitude. He hoped she'd remain that way, but given the life he led, he knew sooner or later she'd be witness to something she wasn't prepared for, and things might change. But for now, he was going to bask in her innocence and his lust for her.

He gently removed her black dress, letting it slip to the floor. He knelt on the lush white carpet and ran his tongue over her legs up to her black lace panties. He pulled them to the side, letting his tongue explore her wet folds.

Elena groaned with delight, letting him know she was enjoying his moves.

He worked his way up to the lace bra that he pulled down to caress her hard nipples. He thumbed each one as Elena rolled her head around while holding onto Tony's sturdy shoulders.

Her hands found their way into Tony's pants, and she worked at pleasuring him, as well. Tony was rock hard, and this turned her on even more.

Tony removed his pants and led her onto the king-size bed. He mounted her and glided his cock over her breasts down to her welcoming entrance, where she was more than ready. His thrusts began slow and easy, then turned harder and faster. Elena dug her fingernails into his back, riding him until she was on the brink of coming. She shouted to Tony. She was ready, and together they came in a joyous reunion, both well-sated.

Ross returned and could see the Mustang was still parked in the back lot. He missed seeing Lamberto's car as it was parked behind a large green hotel dumpster. But Lamberto noticed Ross pull in and alerted Dom, who was snoring loudly. "Wake up! Ross just pulled in!"

Dom jumped. "Who's with him?"

"No one. He's alone," Lamberto said, peering through his binoculars.

"So now we gotta deal with this buffoon!" Dom said.

"Nah, it's gonna make things even better."

Dom looked at his boss with a scrunched-up face. "How so?"

"As soon as Tony drops Elena off, you stall Ross by jumping in front of his car. You'll have your Beretta 93 ready, but you won't need to use it unless he pulls first. Tell him to get the fuck home, or this could end badly."

"And you don't think Ross is armed?"

"I know he is, but you have the element of surprise. While you're dealing with him, I'll deal with Tony. Like I said, I'll work him over lightly, nothing that will put him in the hospital, and you, of course, won't have to shoot Ross."

"Unless this turns ugly," Dom said.

"That happens only if you make it happen. You tell Ross you're stopping him because the boys from the East Side are on his tail."

"Like he's gonna believe that?"

"I have faith in you. This isn't our first rodeo, Dom. You are a schmoozer and one who means business. With your 190-pound frame, no one ever lost with you. Now go back to your nap, and I'll wake you up when we're ready to leave."

Tony was quick to rise after making love to Elena. She sat up, wondering if there was something wrong. "Where are you going? We usually lie with each other for a while." She watched as Tony reached into the pocket of his jacket, pulling out a shiny, wrapped box.

He carried the gift box over to Elena, whose eyes trailed his every move. "What's this?"

"I wanted to give you something special because you are something special to me, Elena."

"I ... I don't know what to say."

"Well, just open it."

Elena tugged on the gold bow gently, then unwrapped the shiny paper, revealing a small black velvet box with the words *Rock Solid Jewelers* on the lid.

Her eyes widened as she held up the solid gold bracelet engraved with the letter L along the outside. "This is … this is too much, Tony! I mean …"

"Try it on, babe."

Elena slipped the bracelet on, and it was a perfect fit for her slender wrist. It glinted as the light from the small chandelier hit it, making it appear as though it was glowing.

"This must have cost a fortune!" Elena said as she turned her wrist around, admiring its beauty.

"Price is nothing when it comes to you. You are worth that and more. And one more thing — I'd like you to move in with me."

"In your father's home?"

"No, it's time I moved out as well. A twenty-five-year-old man shouldn't still be living with his father."

Elena held Tony's gaze and felt shivers run down her spine. She kissed Tony passionately and answered *yes,* thanking him again for the gift.

"But how are we going to …"

Tony put his finger to her swollen lips. "Shh, those are small details. We'll talk about that this week. Let's get you back to Pam's, and you can sleep in. I'll call you in the morning."

As soon as the Mustang left Le Mansion, Ross was in tow, and Lamberto and Dom were not far behind.

Chapter 16

Elena was quiet on the drive home. There wasn't a skirmish, but the bracelet and the invitation to move in with Tony had somehow left previous events in the shadows.

She kissed Tony goodnight, and he reminded her that he'd call her tomorrow to make plans for the move. He also waited until she got in the door and knew she was safe.

He pulled out of Pam's driveway and looked in the rearview mirror to make sure Ross was following him. Sure enough, he was. He thought about all the years that Ross had had his back. Now that he was a grown man, would he still need him, especially if he was taking Elena into his life and moving out?

One block away, Dom was waiting to jump in front of the Town Car. He took one last sip of bourbon out of his flask and was ready. He was riding shotgun and had easy access to the glove compartment. He reached in and grabbed his Beretta 93, slipping it into the holster of his oversized jacket. He hoped he wouldn't need it, but he had to be prepared.

Lamberto spotted the Town Car and signaled for Dom to get out and get into action. He told him he'd pick him up later over at Belucci's market. The streets were dark with few streetlights, and Dom hoped Ross wouldn't run him over. He darted just a few feet away as the Town Car screeched to a halt. He knew Ross was no dummy.

A window was cracked as Dom approached the car. Ross had some words. "What the hell are you doing? Get out of the way, or I'll run you over, you dumb fuck!"

Dom stood frozen. At least the car was stopped, and Lamberto was now on his way to follow Tony.

Ross laid on the horn, but Dom didn't budge, acting as if he was drunk. Ross shouted out his intent to run him over if he didn't move. He had his hand on the car phone, calling Ralph for backup. After seeing Ross pick up the car phone, Dom knew he had to end this charade and hoof it over to the market and wait for Lamberto. If he could avoid a showdown, he would. Ross didn't seem to recognize him, and that was a bonus.

Ross reached Ralph and filled him in on the situation. Ralph told him to forget about the asshole who'd stopped him and go find Tony, so Ross gunned the car and headed for the house.

Lamberto was two cars behind the Mustang and ready for Tony to round the corner on Lansing Ave, then pass him up and slam on the brakes, cutting him off.

It was now in the early hours of the morning, and the neighborhood was quiet. The perfect time to pull the kid out and work him over a bit. He had to be fast, as he didn't know how soon Ross would show up.

Lamberto swerved around the driver's side of the Mustang and stopped at the stop sign, forcing Tony to hit the brakes. Lamberto dashed to the Mustang and opened the driver's side door, pulling Tony out over the curb and onto the lawn of a private residence using his body weight to pull him to the ground.

Tony wrestled with Lamberto, attempting to get the older man off of him. "What the fuck is this?" Tony shouted.

Lamberto had his hands around Tony's neck, but Tony was stronger and much younger, yanking his hands away. Now, Tony had Lamberto on the ground. "Who sent you?"

"I think you damn well know. I don't have to tell you. You need to leave the Donato girl alone, or it won't end well," Lamberto said, holding his gaze with Tony's dark eyes.

"Yeah, we'll see how it ends!" Tony shouted, grabbing Lamberto by his sleeve, sucker punching him, and throwing him into the bushes. Go home and tell your family the Marinettis don't take shit from anyone." Tony was about to pull his Ruger out of his jacket pocket."

Lamberto managed to pull his Beretta from his holster and fired into the air.

Tony attempted to retrieve his gun just as a large man in a bathrobe came out of his front door. "What's going on? I'm calling the police!"

Tony and Lamberto both headed back to their cars, still clutching their weapons, but not before Tony had more words for Lamberto. "I think you know what my family is capable of. We run this town, and if you think for one minute you have any edge on us, you are sadly mistaken and are not far off from being a dead man!"

As Tony peeled away and Lamberto rushed to his car, the homeowner remained standing on his lawn, shaking his head. Lamberto knew he had to go pick up Dom before someone else got to him first.

Tony made it home but still didn't see Ross's car behind him. *Where is he? Was he ambushed, too?* Tony sat in his car, waiting to make sure no one was on the grounds. The iron gate was closed, but that didn't mean they couldn't jump the brick walls that surrounded the property.

Dom sat in front of the large glass doors of Belucci's market waiting for Lamberto. It had been over an hour now, and still no sign of him. "Where the hell is he?" he whispered to himself, scanning the entire lot.

He could see a black van pull into the lot and stop in front of him. The windows were tinted so dark he couldn't see who was driving. Two men got out dressed in grey gas station work attire and grabbed him, throwing him into the back of the van. They put a sack over his head and bound his feet and hands with duct tape. He could hear one of the men make a call to Ralph Marinetti, telling him they'd got one of them. He knew the shit was going down. He wondered if they'd gotten to Lamberto, too.

Lamberto cruised through the market parking lot but didn't see Dom. "Where the hell did he go?" After circling the back lot, he could see something dark lying on the pavement by the huge dumpster. He pulled the car around to the side and got out. On the ground, he found what he feared — a black rose. He knew what that meant, and it wasn't good. Dom was in trouble or possibly dead. It was one of the mob's famous calling cards, so to speak. The Marinettis didn't mess around. He hung his head in his hands. *This can't be happening. We've worked together for fifteen years now. I gotta get home and call for backup.*

The iron gates opened after Ross punched in the code. He pulled in behind the Mustang. Tony and Ralph bounded out of the front door, hearing the car door slam. Ross could see that Tony's neck was red and his clothes all rumpled. "What happened?"

"I was set up! Some old man, whom I'm assuming is from the Russo family, tried to work me over. He warned me to stay away from Elena. And I almost got shot!" Tony had to take a few breaths between words.

"I'm sorry. I was set up, too. Another goon jumped in front of my car to keep me from tailing you. I didn't want to shoot him, and your father told me to just try to follow you."

"I know. Right after your call, I phoned the Bezzeta boys from Campbell to follow that guy. I knew right away this had to do with the Russo family. It's been taken care of."

Ross walked up to Tony and put his arm around him. "I'm sorry. I should have just run that damn fuck over!"

"You did what I told you to do," Ralph said.

Tony shot back, "I don't want Elena to get hurt! I had no idea her family was in the business! I don't want anyone in her family to get hurt."

"But this ain't over yet. These men *are* from Elena's family and the dark side of it, like it or not. It's her mother's side that's trouble, the Russo family," Ralph said.

"The Russo family is in the business?" Tony asked, looking at Ross and back to his father.

"And did you honestly think she would tell you?" Ross asked.

Tony shook his head, still in denial. "I think I just need to get some rest."

"Well, I know your father will want to speak to you, but it can wait until morning," Ross patted Tony on the back.

Before Tony walked in the door, he turned to Ross, "If I have to leave town to get away from all this shit, I will, and I'll take Elena with me. She's innocent and has nothing to do with a crime family. My father will pull shit out of his ass just to keep me away from Elena."

Ralph told Tony to go upstairs and get some rest, as he needed to have a few words with Ross.

"This means war. We gotta step up our game now," Ralph said, scanning his vast property for any sign of intruders.

"Yeah?" Ross asked, his hands on his hips.

"Yeah, we take out the Donato girl this week," Ralph said, patting Ross on the back.

Chapter 17

No sooner than Lamberto closed his front door, he grabbed an ice pack and was on the phone with some of his other buddies up in the Cleveland area, informing them of what went down tonight. There were at least three men from the Amato family who were trusted friends of the family. They informed him they'd be down Monday to make plans and find out what happened to Dom. Now he had to call Fran, and this was going to be even harder. She'd known Dom since her high school days. They grew up on the same street. It was Fran who brought him in to work with Lamberto, knowing they'd been friends since childhood.

It was approaching five in the morning, but Lamberto knew he had to get hold of Fran to tell her the news.

"This isn't good, not good at all. Do whatever it takes to find out what happened to Dom," Fran said in an authoritative tone. "How is Tony?"

"He's okay, just a bit bruised. Nothing a few band-aids and a good soak won't fix."

"And you?" Fran asked.

"Just a swollen nose. I've got an ice pack on it now."

"Good to hear it's nothing serious. But who knows who's next? I've got to get Elena to reason with me. We both know it may be her next," Fran said, pushing the button on her coffee machine, feeling the need for caffeine.

Lamberto promised to keep her posted on the search for Dom and reassured Fran that he and his buddies from Cleveland would be in touch.

Elena opened her eyes as the first rays of sunlight peeked through the green linen drapes, as she lay on the large overstuffed couch in Pam's living room. She glanced at the clock over the fireplace and saw it was 7 a.m. It was Sunday, and she had told her mom she'd be home sometime today. The house was quiet; Pam was probably still sleeping, and her parents had most likely gone to early Mass.

She lay back down on the couch and covered herself up with the soft afghan. She didn't feel like facing her mother again today. There were no hassles at Pam's, but she knew she had to go home at some point. There were plans to make. She didn't have to give a second thought to moving in with Tony.

Pam tiptoed into the living room, not wanting to wake her friend, but could see she was already awake. She sat on the edge of the couch. "Hey, you okay?"

Elena sat up, still clinging to the afghan. "I'm more than okay. Tony asked me to move in with him."

Pam couldn't believe her ears. "You sure this is what you want?"

"It's all I've ever wanted, ever since I met Tony. And you know what? I don't give a rat's ass if he or his dad is in the mob."

"Well, all I want is for you to be safe and happy," Pam said as she opened the drapes slightly to peer out the window.

Elena stood up. "Don't tell me you're paranoid now, too."

The kitchen phone rang. Pam answered; it was Tony calling. Elena wrapped the afghan around herself and padded into the kitchen as Pam handed her the phone. "Hi, Tony." Her voice was still sleepy, but she was excited to take his call.

Tony's voice had an urgent tone to it, and Elena listened intently as he told her all that had happened to him last night after he dropped her off.

She couldn't believe someone had done that to him, and her intuition told her she might know who that someone was. "I ... I'm so sorry, Tony. I don't blame you if you never want to see me again. I'd never want anyone to hurt you!

Elena was shocked to hear the news and could tell from his voice that he was more than upset. "Look, Elena, I don't know what's going on yet, but the rumor has it that the man who attacked me was somehow related to your family. But they won't scare me. No one on earth will keep us apart. I've spoken to my dad, and he says he'll ramp up his men to make sure it doesn't happen again. I'm not letting a few geriatric henchmen scare me."

"This can't — I mean it won't."

"Look, I told my father I'm leaving with you soon, and I want nothing to do with his business. It's over!"

Elena went quiet to take a breath, knowing Tony was getting more upset with every spoken word. "Just tell me when you want to leave, and I'll be ready. I haven't spoken to my folks yet, but I will and soon."

Tony told Elena to be ready by the weekend. She'd have to finish up her classes at school through Friday, and they'd plan to leave by Saturday. He knew it would have to be at Pam's house again because he was sure he would be off limits on her property again.

"Listen, Elena, you're all I care about. My father got into this business years ago — he was born into it. I'm sick of it. It's time you and I left as soon as possible for Cleveland and leave this all behind."

Elena fell silent for a moment, trying to comprehend all of this. "But how can we just pick up and leave?"

"Not to worry. Ross will help us. He's on my side. He can make arrangements for an apartment and take care of shit. This is what he does."

"But I have one week left for school, then spring break. What should I do?"

"Finish out your week, then we leave. You can enroll in Cleveland State University. I've got money — lots of it. My dad likes you, and I'm sure I can get him to see the light."

Elena listened but knew there would be no light her mother would see, only darkness.

Tony discussed plans for them to meet at Lanterman's Mill in Mill Creek Park on Friday after her last afternoon class. He'd have all the details ready for her.

But for now, she had to pack up her things and get home to face her folks with the details she knew they weren't going to like. But first, she'd address the attack on Tony, possibly started by that scumbag, Lamberto.

Chapter 18

Pam dropped Elena off at home at a time when Elena was sure her parents would be at mass. She needed to pack some things, clear her head, and prepare for another face-off with her mother. This one was going to be harder than the others. She was leaving — and for good.

The sound of the garage door opening told Elena that her parents were home from Mass. She tiptoed downstairs. Her father was the first to enter the kitchen. He greeted her with a hug, "Glad to have you back. I've missed you, but I knew you were in good hands over at Pam's."

Fran was right behind him, and by the look on her mother's face, Elena knew harsh words were ahead, even with the tight grip she had on her husband. "Yes, it's good to have you back. We have to have a serious talk. Let me put on the coffee first, then we can all chat."

Elena kept a tight lip and wasn't about to delve into her news of leaving until she heard what her mother had to say.

Fran sat at the table and took Elena's hand as Salvatore poured them both a cup of coffee. "I have some very bad news. I ... I don't know how to tell you this."

"What? What's going on?"

"It's Dominic. Dominic Terruza."

"What about him?"

"He's missing and ... probably ... dead!"

"Wh … what do you mean?" Elena shook her head. She was shocked; Dom was like a member of the family, a best friend to Lamberto.

"Yes, you heard me. We've had a report that he's most likely been taken by your boyfriend's father's mobsters. And you know this won't end well."

"Well, I'm sorry to hear this, but you don't know for sure. And how would you know how it will end?" Elena gave her mother a quizzical look. "And I have something to discuss with you!"

She went on to tell her mother and father how Tony was attacked. "From the description Tony gave me, I know it was most likely Lamberto or one of his goons! Who else in this town looks like a bulldog?"

Salvatore put his hand on his wife's shoulder. "You didn't, did you?"

Fran squared her shoulders and shot back in defiance. "Yes, it was Lamberto! I had to resort to this because no one would listen, you nor our daughter!"

Elena shot up from her chair. "You see what you've done! You had your scumbag of a cousin almost kill Tony, and now your cousin's best friend may be dead! And you know what, I wouldn't doubt for a minute that you're more involved with the mob than Tony or his father is!"

"I won't tolerate that kind of talk in this house!" Fran shook her finger at Elena.

"Well, you won't have to for long. I'll be out of here this weekend," Elena snapped back.

Salvatore came to his daughter's side, taking her hand, and pleaded with her to stay. "This won't solve anything."

But Elena marched upstairs, leaving her folks to digest her words.

Salvatore sat with his wife as they discussed their next move. He begged her to call Lamberto and tell him there would be no more attempts to interfere with their daughter's relationship, but Fran was far too upset over the disappearance of Dom and Elena's attitude. If anything, she told her husband she would call Lamberto to ramp up the search for Dom.

Lamberto had just gotten off the phone with Rocky Amato, one of the head henchmen from Cleveland, whom he had reached out to for help with getting information on Dom's whereabouts. The news wasn't good. From insider sources, Rocky had to tell Lamberto that Dom was dead — there was no mistaking it. The news hit him hard, but it would hit Fran harder. He decided to take a ride to clear his head before he made that call.

Elena spent most of the time in her room making plans and going through her things, deciding what to pack. Her nerves were on edge, and she was not really focusing on what she was tossing into her suitcase. Her college books would fill another entire suitcase. Mainly, she thought about Tony and his safety. She knew she needed space from her mother as things were going from bad to worse. News of Dominic had turned up the fire in her mother, and she was well aware of how she might retaliate.

She knew Tony wouldn't dare call the house. The only way she'd see him this week was by meeting him at Mill Creek Park. It was her secret sanctuary. After two hours of packing, she sat on her bed, her brain running all sorts of possible scenarios that might transpire on Saturday. There were a lot of 'what ifs' on her mind.

Lamberto came back from his ride and was ready to call his cousin, but then decided he should deliver the news in person. It was nearing 3 p.m., and he hoped it was a good time to visit her, if there ever was a good time.

Fran answered the door, and from the look on her cousin's face, she knew the news was not good. Lamberto came in and removed his fedora, setting it on the entry table. He put his arm around her waist as they walked over to the living room sofa. Salvatore had just entered the room and sat in the overstuffed chair across from them.

"Would anyone like a glass of wine?" he asked.

Fran just shook her head, and Lamberto waved him off.

"Where is Elena?" Lamberto asked.

"Upstairs in her room," Fran replied.

"Maybe she shouldn't come down," Lamberto said, glancing at the stairs. There were no mincing words. "Yes, I've had news from one of the Amato boys, Dom is dead."

Elena knew Lamberto was in the house and opened her bedroom door to listen to the conversation. *Damn, I want to rip his throat out! How could Mom and this monster do this to Tony?*

She tiptoed further down into the hall, wanting to hear more of their conversation.

"You know, none of this would have happened if not for that toxic relationship Elena is in," Fran said. "The Marinettis have bad juju. You and I both know that family was cursed by an old gypsy over in Italy years ago."

Salvatore came and sat beside his wife. "Now that's just an old legend, but I know more violence begets violence, and we've had enough already in this family. And now we just got the news that Elena is moving in with Tony."

Fran looked to her husband with tears in her eyes, "We can't let this happen, and we won't!"

"Let me take care of this. I'll do it for Dom," Lamberto said, taking her hand, which was shaking.

Hearing those words, Elena knew she had to get to Pam's and call Tony. Fuck staying here the week; she had to get out as soon as possible.

<h1 style="text-align:center">Chapter 19</h1>

There was a knock on Elena's bedroom door. In a gentle tone, her father said, "Elena, please, let's talk. I've calmed your mother down, and I believe she's willing to come to her senses about all of this."

Elena opened the door to a man who had looked as though he'd been crying. Even though he had a rough exterior and strong, dark looks, he had a gentle soul. He put his hand around her waist, and they walked over to sit on the edge of the bed.

Salvatore spoke first, wanting to get his words out before Elena had a chance to speak. "I know how you feel, and you have every right to feel this way. Your mother and I have talked and ..."

"Is Lamberto still here?"

"No, he's gone."

"Good. I don't ever want to see him again. For what he did to Tony!"

"I know, my dear, I know. But I've reasoned with your mother and convinced her that she, or anyone in her family, is never to harm Tony or members of his family. She knows she risks the possibility of losing you forever."

Elena was silent, just shaking her head.

Her father begged her to put the suitcases away and think about staying, but Elena insisted she planned to move out, despite hurting her father. She blamed her mother for trying to ruin her life.

Salvatore stood and walked toward the door. He turned around when Elena called to him. "I love you, Dad, and want you to know I'll always be in touch with you, but for Mom … I just don't know when I can talk to her again. Not now, maybe never."

Soon after Lamberto arrived home, he was on the phone with Rocky Amato. He'd informed him of a more advanced plan to do away with Tony. Things had to speed up. He knew from Fran that Tony and Elena were planning to leave this weekend, so they'd have to intercept him sometime on Thursday of this week.

Lamberto knew Tony's route; it was the same one he ran for his father every Thursday. He would transfer money from Ralph's illegal betting at the Maple Lane Dry Cleaners over to Rock Solid Jewelers. Ross never followed him on those days, as John Carino's boys always had a lookout blocks away from the store.

Rocky had a run-in with the Carino boys years ago and always welcomed assignments to seek further revenge, but he questioned how far they would go to make Tony disappear.

"Look, Rocky, it's simple. We let the word slip out that the Feds are within a few blocks of the jewelry store before we head out, and then we move in and rush Tony before he gets into his car."

"Yeah, how you gonna manage that one? You got more leverage now than the last time I worked with you?"

"I've got my plants in there, Rock … ones who owe me a favor."

"So where do we take the kid?"

"Not the usual. Everyone in this town knows where we hide the bodies. It's most likely where Dom was dumped. I still can't get over that one. I'll get my revenge this way, and hopefully we'll be done with the Marinettis for good."

"And I hear you got some new toys. You gotta share, you know," Rocky said.

"You can bet on it, my friend."

Lamberto ended his call and phoned Fran to let her know everything was in place.

Elena's alarm blared loud and clear early Tuesday morning. She had an early class and had to get her head straight about getting through the week and just playing nice with her mom. No use in starting up another argument.

She went down for coffee as usual, just as her mom was leaving for work. Her dad had already left. Her mom had a few minutes to sit with her before heading out the door. She ran a hand through her ruffled pixie cut. "Look, Elena, I know your dad spoke to you last night. Whether you believe it or not, I've resolved to accept Tony because I don't want to lose you. I want you to be happy, and if living with Tony makes you happy, then that's what I want."

Elena held her gaze with her mom, not really believing her words. "Thanks, Ma. I'm glad for your support, but I plan on being out of here before the weekend. I'm moving in with Tony."

Fran knew her daughter would do whatever the hell she wanted, whether or not she had her support. She hugged Elena and told her to have a good morning at school.

Elena took a deep breath and watched her mother close the kitchen door behind her. She poured herself a cup of coffee and grabbed a Danish. She stared out the kitchen window at the shrine of Our Lady in the backyard, which her mother had built the first year they moved into the house. *For such a Christian woman, how could she and her family ever hurt anyone, or kill anyone, for God's sake?*

Chapter 20

Elena was just about to leave the house when the kitchen phone rang. *Could it be Tony?* Her heart thumped in her chest. It was Pam. "My friend, I have a problem."

"What's wrong?"

"The car won't start, and I have a class at 9."

"No problem. If you don't mind leaving early, I'll swing by and pick you up. Be there in fifteen."

Wearing her favorite worn jeans and a Pink Floyd T-shirt, she packed up her school supplies into her school bag and loaded her Dodge Challenger, then went back into the house to grab her yellow rain slicker. Rain was in the forecast for today. The morning traffic was light as she headed toward Pam's. Thoughts of skipping her classes ran through her head. She wanted to turn the car around and head toward Tony's house, but that wasn't an option, as she had an oral presentation in her first class and her friend needed a ride as well.

Thoughts of Tony brought a small smile to her face. She knew things were going to change fast, before anyone in her family had a chance to hurt him again. The weekend would come soon enough, and she'd be on a new journey with Tony.

Pam was already waiting outside as Elena pulled into her driveway. She had her backpack and was carrying her yellow rain slicker, the same as Elena's. "Hey, lady, ya got good taste," Elena said, eyeing the slicker with the hood.

"We sure do. Remember, we bought them together while shopping a few months ago," Pam said as she threw her things onto the backseat and took the passenger side seat, reaching over to hug her friend. "Oh, you saved me!"

"Look who's talking. You've saved me more times than I can think," Elena shot back.

As Elena pulled onto Youngstown Poland Road, Pam called her attention to a black Town Car behind them. "You don't think ..."

"Now we can't get paranoid. It's nothing." Elena quickly changed the conversation to the dark clouds looming ahead. "Looks like that rain is coming."

Ralph Marinetti had just gotten off the phone with Ross Vincenzi. Everything was set for taking Elena today after her last class at the university. He and Max Tussi would ambush her as she walked to her car. Ralph had decided to leave John to mind the jewelry store. He didn't need three men to take care of one 110-pound girl. Ross would inject her with the sedative, then drive up to Lake Erie, where her body would be dumped. He took a deep breath and thought about how he would finally get revenge for his cousin's death and save his son from getting involved with the Russo family. *Tony won't blame me. He knows there are too many other families here in town that would love to see the Russos fall. I'm doing him a favor,* he thought as he gazed out the huge window from his office, taking in the dark clouds overhead.

Max had just pulled into Ross's driveway when it started to pour. He didn't want to get out of the car, so he laid on the horn. After three beeps, there was no sign of Ross. "Where the hell is he?" Max was just about to run to the door when Ross came bounding out of the door and opened the passenger side. He was soaked and still in his pajama pants.

Max gave a stern look to Ross. "What's going on with you? You ready to roll?"

"I couldn't sleep all night. I just can't do this. You know I love Tony and feel like a second father to him. He loves that girl."

"You shittin' me? You turning into a pussy?" Max shot back. "The boss ain't gonna like this."

"I don't care what he likes. I'm not going through with this, and if it means leaving you and Ralph for good, so be it. You're on your own, here." Ross opened the door and ran back into the house.

"Fuck him!" Max used the car phone to call Ralph and tell him the news. He told Max he'd call John, who'd meet him in the Branson Market parking lot by the university and have another injection ready. He'd be there to help Max.

Arriving so early, Elena easily found an open spot on the lower level of the parking deck, being so early. She parked the car and looked in her rearview mirror. "See, no black Town Car, Pam. Relax." Before she opened the car door, she turned to her friend, "I know you have a later class, so I'll wait in the library for you."

"Thanks, Elena. I know I can always count on you."

"Anything for you. You know we've had each other's backs since third grade, girl. You know I love you. "

Both girls headed to their classes, as thunder boomed, thunder that was louder than normal. Elena glanced at the sky as she approached the art building, her slicker on her arm. She had goosebumps. Not one to be afraid of storms, but this one had a strange energy to it. She shook it off and opened the huge glass door to the art building.

Elena was nervous about her presentation of the watercolor she'd done of the covered bridge at Mill Creek Park. She knew it was not her best but hoped it would bring her a passing grade.

Pam headed toward her literature class and found a notice on the door:

Class Cancelled
Will Resume on Friday

There was no explanation, but with Mr. Hawkins being an older professor, Pam wondered if he'd been ill. She headed toward the library to sit and wait for Elena. She threw on her slicker as it started to pour; she was going to have to run to the library building on the far end of campus.

Walking through the library doors, Pam let the smell of old books engulf her. The place was mostly empty. Most of the students had ditched classes and gone home due to the weather. Some of the older historical novels that she loved were on the lower level, so she descended the stairs to the basement. Two boys were sitting at the back table. After an hour, she decided to head back to the car, where she left a literature book she needed to do some homework. She headed out to the parking deck, pulling the slicker over her head and ducking between the huge raindrops.

Max and John sat in Max's car right around the corner from Elena's car, waiting for her to emerge. Max knew he had to do this with or without Ross. He wouldn't let his boss down. He had his Colt Hammerless, just in case he had to deal with any interference.

When Pam reached the silver Challenger, she whispered a prayer that it would be unlocked. Elena never locked it — an awful habit she'd tried to break her of a hundred times. But she got lucky today.

The door opened. Her book still lay on the backseat.

She turned as she heard a screech tearing through the lot.

A black car skidded sideways, tires smoking. Two masked men burst out and charged.

"What the hell —?"

She dropped her school bag and locked herself in the car.

Too late.

John approached the car to see a girl in her yellow slicker crouched down in the front seat.

She screamed, scooting herself far against the passenger side door, her hand on the handle, ready to jump out, but John began smashing in the driver's side window with a baseball bat. Glass shattered everywhere.

He'd come prepared, grabbed both her arms, hauling her off to the backseat. Pam kicked, clawed, tried to scream, but his grip crushed the air from her lungs. John removed her slicker, holding her down as Max was ready to administer the drug.

He moved fast — gloved hands, cold eyes. A syringe flashed.

"No —!" Pam continued to fight back, but she was no match for two big men.

The needle plunged into her right arm.

Fire. Then ice.

Her strength drained instantly. The world tilted.

John was ready to move her body into the trunk of Max's car, but Max had other orders. "Let's let her lie here. We need to make sure the drug has taken effect."

But she was already fading. Sound muffled, her vision tunneling.

Her body went slack.

Max leaned into the back seat and picked her up. She was a dead weight. "Sleep well, my dear girl," he muttered just before he had her halfway out of the backseat.

Then — another engine. Tires screaming.

Max turned.

A silver Cutlass roared into the lot and fishtailed behind his car.

"Fuck. No!"

The driver's door flew open. A short man in a fedora stepped out, bulldog face set in stone, Beretta 93 already raised.

The Lamb.

Max didn't make it two steps. Lamberto slammed into him, driving him hard into the pavement. Air exploded from Max's lungs.

"You really thought you'd get away with this?" Lamberto snarled, jamming the gun into his face. "Where's Elena, you piece of shit?"

Rocky — tall, bushy mustache bristling—dragged John into a brutal chokehold near the hood.

Max said nothing.

Lamberto answered with his fists. Bone against bone. Again. Again. Blood sprayed across the asphalt.

Rocky left John gasping and told Lamberto to look in the Challenger.

Pam lay motionless in the back seat; her slicker had been removed. Lamberto studied the girl's pale face and motionless body.

"Jesus."

Not Elena.

Pam.

He'd seen her at family barbecues. Laughing. Alive. She was Elena's best friend.

Now she was gray and still.

He checked her neck. Pulse — faint. Thready.

"No blood," he muttered, relief and fury colliding. "She's alive."

He looked up. "Rocky! He grabbed the wrong girl — it's not Elena! Thank God!"

Rocky froze mid-swing. "Who is it?"

"It's Pam. Elena's friend. Weak pulse. Real weak." Lamberto's voice sharpened. "Get in the car. Use the car phone and call an ambulance. Give them the lot, the make, everything. Move!"

Rocky sprinted to the Cutlass, radioing it in, then rushed back and planted a knee into Max's spine, keeping him pinned.

Lamberto stripped off Pam's slicker, checking her breathing. Shallow. Slowing.

Rage snapped.

He crossed back to Max and drove a boot into his ribs. Once. Twice. Max coughed up blood, wheezing.

"You almost killed an innocent girl, you animal!"

Rocky's Ruger stayed trained on John, who sagged against the car, barely conscious. For a moment, Rocky looked ready to end them both right there.

Not here," Lamberto said quietly. "I've got a better idea."

The distant wail of sirens was heard in the distance.

Lamberto hauled Max upright. "In the car!"

They dragged him to the Cutlass and shoved him into the backseat. Max barely resisted, half-conscious and bleeding.

John staggered toward his own car, broken and stumbling.

Rocky slid behind the wheel. Lamberto climbed in beside him. He had a call to make.

The Cutlass peeled out just as the first siren turned into the lot — leaving behind the wrong victim, fighting for her life in the backseat of a silent car.

"What's the plan now, boss?"

"We drive him out to the countryside and leave him there. From the looks of it, he won't make it."

"What? I was dying to see Lake Erie again," Rocky joked.

"Nah, this is a dire warning to him and his goons. Next time we do him in for good, besides, the cops will be here soon." Lamberto said as Rocky hit the gas, peeling out of the parking lot.

Chapter 21

Lamberto made another call while Rocky drove. He wanted to let his cousin know Elena was fine, but her friend was in serious condition. He had to call her at her work number. He also told her he was going to finish this situation once and for all, and he had Fran's blessing.

"But where is Elena? Did you see her?" Fran's voice was frantic.

"No, we couldn't wait. I'm sure she's in class. Her car is still here. The police will surely want to do a sweep of the car. The passenger side window is smashed in. Max must have mistaken Pam for Elena. I called for an ambulance. It's on the way."

"Dear Lord, have mercy on us all!" Fran cried.

"Don't worry, Fran, this will shut up the entire Marinetti family. This is over with!"

As soon as Fran got off the phone with her cousin, she informed her boss that she had a family emergency. She drove to the university to look for her daughter.

Elena finished her coffee, walked out of the cafeteria, and headed toward the parking deck. The rain had abated, and she carried her slicker along with her school bag.

She could hear a siren coming from the parking garage. *I wonder what's going on,* she thought as she quickened her step.

Coming closer, she saw two orderlies carrying Pam out on a gurney and into the ambulance. She dropped her bag and ran up to them. "Hey! That's my friend! What's going on?"

One of the younger orderlies informed her that they'd gotten a call about a young woman passed out in a car — her car!

"I'm coming with you!" Elena shouted as she climbed into the back of the ambulance, holding Pam's hand, never noticing the smashed window. Her friend was still out of it as she watched the other middle-aged medic hook up Pam to a heart monitor and check all her vitals.

"Where are you taking her?"

"We are en route to North Side Hospital, Miss. We've already called ahead, and they are waiting for her at the emergency," the younger man said, brushing the hair out of his eyes. "We've also alerted the police. We noticed a smashed window in the car as well. Looks like it may have been an attack. And we'll need her name and emergency contacts by the way."

Elena nodded and provided all the necessary information they needed. She held on tight to her friend's hand. "It's going to be all right. I'm not leaving you." She looked down at her friend's ashen face. *What on earth happened to you?* Suddenly, dark thoughts filled her head. *No! Why would she come back to the car and who broke in?*

The portly middle-aged orderly reported that Pam had appeared to be drugged, but further testing at the hospital would be able to confirm the cause of her condition.

Elena squeezed her friend's hand. "You're going to be just fine," she whispered in her ear.

Fran reached the parking deck and made a few rounds until she found Elena's car. She parked and walked up to the car to peek inside. Elena was nowhere in sight, but she noticed her bag and slicker were lying in the parking deck, as well as the smashed window. Shards of glass were strewn all over the front seat. "Where the hell is she? Who did this?"

Bending down to collect her things, she noticed blood stains on the back end of the car. *I pray these aren't Pam's or Elena's. Why didn't Lamberto know where my daughter was?*

As the ambulance approached the hospital, two nurses rushed out, and the automatic doors swung open, ready for the gurney to be wheeled inside. Elena moved right along with them.

Right before they wheeled Pam into the back room, a middle-aged orderly informed Elena that she had to stay in the waiting room. Elena cried and protested, but understood these were their rules.

No sooner had the doors to the private entrance closed than she scanned the room for a phone and headed to the corner where there was one for public use sitting on a side table. She had calls to make. She dialed her mother's number, and then she'd have to call Pam's folks. And finally, she had to call Tony. She was angry and worried at the same time. She felt dizzy and wondered if she'd be the next one to need a gurney.

Elena's home phone rang and rang. *Damn! She's at work, so is Dad!* She fished out her wallet, where she had written down her emergency numbers, and found her mother's work number. An elderly lady answered, whom Elena knew was her mother's boss. "No, Elena. She left; said she had a family emergency." Now Elena's head was really spinning. *What the hell is going on?* She tried to call her dad, but reached his boss, who informed her he was out on the floor in the warehouse.

She hung up the phone, feeling a bit faint, and knew she needed water. There was a vending machine in the room with soda, but no water. She opted for a Coke, reasoning that maybe her blood sugar was low. After a few sips, she started to feel a bit better and stared at the phone, deciding if she was ready to call Pam's folks or not. She knew her mother didn't work and would be home. Hell, she had to call. Her folks had the right to know. She took another gulp of her soda and was ready to call Pam's mother when Ruth walked through the doors. "Where's my daughter?"

Elena rushed up to her. "She's back with the doctors now. How did you know?"

"The nurse's station called me shortly after she was brought in."

The woman at the desk had told her that she could go back into the room and see her daughter. Just then, a tall, stern-looking doctor emerged from the double doors, informing Ruth that her daughter was going to be fine. He told her they are running bloodwork now, and she is slowly waking up."

Ruth looked at the doctor, 'Waking up? What caused this?"

"We aren't sure yet, but there seems to be no injuries other than a small puncture mark to her arm."

"Puncture mark?" Ruth's face turned pale.

The doctor seemed vague, not wanting to disclose too much information until all the tests were completed.

Elena hugged Ruth and told her to go on back to be with her daughter, but she'd remain in the waiting room for word on her friend's condition.

Why on earth would someone do this? Pam didn't take drugs! She never mentioned anyone who had it out for her. And just then, dark thoughts invaded her brain. *No! It couldn't be! There's no reason for anyone to hurt her!*

Elena had one more call to make, and that was to Tony. If his family was involved in this, she knew it would be all over for them, but she had to be sure.

After leaving the university parking lot, Fran figured her daughter would most likely be with Pam, and that they would have transported her to the nearest hospital, which was North Side. She now headed toward the hospital in hopes that Elena would be there and unharmed.

Chapter 22

Elena paced the waiting room, sweat pouring down her face. She finally got up the nerve to phone Tony. Luckily, she got him on the third ring. "I was almost ready to hang up," Elena said in a shaky tone.

"What's wrong?"

Elena took a deep breath and informed him of the situation with Pam. "You have to come clean with me. I mean, my best friend was almost killed! I have to know if your father's goons were involved."

Tony was silent for a moment, and never hearing Elena speak this way about his father had him stunned. "I can promise you he had nothing to do with this."

Elena started to sob, and Tony had no way of consoling her without being with her. "Look, I'm going to speak to my father now, and I'll get back to you. Just let me know where you are."

Elena gave him the name of the hospital and hoped his call would confirm that Tony's dad had no part in Pam's attack.

The double doors at the front entrance opened, and Fran walked through, breathless. She spotted her daughter sitting over in the corner with her head in her hands. "Elena! Are you alright?"

Elena looked up, tears welling in her eyes. "I'm … I'm not. Pam was attacked this morning!"

Fran swallowed hard, trying to find the right words to comfort her daughter. She couldn't reveal now what she already knew, but there would be a time and place for that, but not here.

"So, what do we know about Pam's condition so far?" Fran asked, taking a seat beside Elena.

"The doctor said there was a puncture wound in her arm, and it was mostly from an injection. They are running tests now."

Fran sat there taking a deep breath before she had to ask her daughter a most sensitive question: "Was Pam taking any drugs?"

Elena stood up, her face red with rage, "Drugs! What? You have to be kidding me! You know Pam would never do a thing like this. How dare you! If anything, this had to do with your family's ongoing feud with other mobsters. I know that your cousin is still involved in crime. If I find out he had anything to do with this, I'll never speak to you again!"

Fran tried to pull her daughter in closer, but Elena pulled away, screaming, "Don't you touch me! I can't wait until I move in with Tony."

A security guard, hearing the ruckus, marched over. "Now, ladies, you can't be quarreling here. If you need to settle something, I will have to ask you to step outside."

Elena apologized to the man and agreed to calm down.

No sooner had Ruth walked through the door than Elena ran up to her. "What's the news? Is Pam going to be alright?"

Ruth put her hand on Elena's shoulder, "Let's go sit down, and I'll tell you what the doctor just told me. I see your mother is here now."

Fran got up and hugged Ruth. "I'm so sorry. Just let me know if there's anything I can do."

All three ladies sat down as Ruth explained what the doctor had told her.

"According to the tests, they found traces of Midazolam in her bloodstream. They put her on an IV to flush the drug out of her system. They'll keep her overnight just for observation."

"Dear Lord!" Elena cried. "Who did this? Why?"

"I don't know, but the police are at the university now checking your car, and then they will come here to question you and Pam, once she is fully awake and coherent," Ruth said.

With the mention of the police, Fran's face turned pale once again. "I'm sure they'll all figure this out soon."

She turned to Elena, informing her that she had to leave to get back to work, but knew Elena would be in good hands here. She couldn't risk being here when the police arrived, knowing they knew all too well that the Russo family was still active in mob activity.

Ruth informed Fran that she would drive Elena home later.

Elena thought about her car in the parking lot and wondered how she'd get it home, but reasoned she wouldn't have to worry about it until the police had finished up what they needed to do. The smashed window was the least of her concerns.

Fran turned and walked through the glass doors, minus a hug from her daughter.

Elena and Ruth sat back down. Ruth wanted to ask Elena a few questions before the police arrived, but she had to call her husband first. "Please tell me everything you know that happened this morning, and for God's sake, please tell me what's been going on with you and that Tony Marinetti. It's no secret you've been seeing him. You've stayed at our home, knowing your mother thought he was trouble. I hope to God he and his family had nothing to do with this!"

Elana shook her head, "I don't think so. I'm waiting for a call from Tony soon as he is done speaking with his father, but I've heard nothing yet."

Ruth nodded and suggested they head down to the hospital cafeteria to get something to eat.

Driving home, all Fran could think about was what Lamberto had told her. She was relieved Salvatore wouldn't be home when she arrived — it would give her time to prepare for what she had to say. He was working the night shift and would get home late.

The phone was ringing as she entered the house. It was Lamberto. He was calling from a bar up in Cleveland. "It's done. We took care of Max."

"You killed him?"

"No, we beat him up pretty bad and dumped his body out in a field in Columbiana. John was in bad shape, too, but was able to get away before the cops came. Yes, he was hired by Ralph to do to Elena what accidentally happened to Pam. I know this is hard to take, but it's the God's truth."

"And where was Ross Vincenzi, Ralph's right-hand man?"

"Not there. I know it's strange," Lamberto said.

Fran searched for words, "I can't deal with this, can't deal with losing Elena. I'm sick to my stomach. Salvatore doesn't even know yet."

"So, tell me, what do you want me to do now?" Lamberto waited for a response.

"End it. End it soon before Elena is killed. I need both of these men to meet their maker, and I'm sure it won't be the maker they hoped to see."

Chapter 23

Tony could hear his father on the phone in his study. His husky voice carried, and he was speaking in Italian, but Tony could make out the mention of Max Tussi and John Carino's names. Tony knew Max was one of his father's raunchy henchmen.

John had called from his car phone, informing Ralph of what had gone down in the parking garage. "Max was beaten up pretty bad, but I don't know where he is," John said.

"What? Does he have his pager?" Ralph asked.

"I'm sure he does, but I haven't heard anything as of yet."

"And you're okay? Don't need to see a doctor?"

"I'm good. Let's just find Max."

Tony walked into the study ready to confront his father on the issue with Pam's accident, but found Ross leaving, and by the look on Ross's face, the man was quite upset.

Tony followed Ross to the front door, trying to find out what had happened.

Ross turned around to face Tony, "Look, son, I told your father I'm quitting. It's time this old guy retired and found that place by the beach in Florida where I've always wanted to live. Besides, my sister is there. "

Tony grabbed hold of his right arm. "What's wrong, Ross? This isn't like you. You've been like a second father to me. Were you aware of that attack on Elena's girlfriend, Pam, this morning? Tell me the truth, I deserve to know." Tony held Ross's gaze.

Ross shook his head. "There are things I can't tell you now, and I think you know that. Go and speak to your father. He's the one you need to question."

Tony could tell just by Ross's mannerisms that his father and his goons were in on Pam's attack. He stood on the front porch watching Ross head toward a strange black Buick where a man was waiting for him. He followed him to the car. "Will I ever see you again?"

Ross hugged Tony. "I'll call you before I leave for Florida. Take care of yourself and go and have a wonderful life with Elena."

As soon as the Buick pulled away, Tony headed back into the house to confront his father, who was still in the study.

He took a seat in the high-backed chair across from his father's desk, locking eyes with his father. Ralph ended the call, aware of the serious look on his son's face. "It's a bit too early to get so serious, son. What's bothering you?"

Tony leaned onto the large oak desk, resting his elbows, eyes dead set on his father's deep browns. "I want to know if your men had anything to do with the attempted murder of Pam Ramone this morning?"

"You've got to be kidding me. Why would I —"

"Why wouldn't you? I know you've had an ongoing feud with the Russo family for decades, and word is out that your men did away with Dominic Terruzza, a family friend of the Russo family. So don't lie to me!"

"Look, son, I had no connection to either of these events. I've been too busy with upcoming work that I don't have time to get my hands dirty with petty crimes."

"Petty — like an attempted murder of Elena's best friend? Pam was nearly killed by mistake. These men meant to hurt Elena. They got the wrong girl, and I know this won't stop until they get the right girl, and I know it's Elena!" Tony pounded his fist on the desk.

Ralph stood up and walked toward his son, placing his hand on his shoulder. "I really like Elena and know you are in love with her. Why would I do this sort of thing?"

Tony pushed away. "I know you're lying. You think I don't know how many crimes you've committed in this city and others? I'm not stupid! And to think you have gotten me involved in your petty money laundering and betting gigs over the years. And Ross — now you've lost a good man. He told me he's quitting, and I damn well know why! Well, it's over. I told you I'm leaving with Elena, and I wash my hands of everything I've ever done for you."

Ralph followed his son toward the front door. "Listen, don't leave, you're just upset. We can take off for a short holiday in Palermo. You need to get away, clear your head."

"Yes, I do need to get away, and from you!" Tony stormed out the front door, heading to his car to head to North Side Hospital to see Elena.

He walked by the old Town Car and knew Ross would no longer be their main driver. *Ross may have done some dirty work for Dad, but I could see it in his face. The man is done with all of this, and possibly this assignment was one that he realized he just couldn't bring himself to do.*

Just as John pulled into the driveway of his home, his car phone was ringing. It was Max. "Where the hell are you?"

Max's voice was weak but audible. "I'm at a farmhouse in Columbiana. I just about crawled to this place, and the nice lady here let me use her phone."

"Give me the address, and I'll be on my way. Do you need an ambulance?"

"No ... I'm okay, just need some rest."

John was on the phone with Ralph, informing him of Max's condition. Ralph ordered John to bring him to the house, as he would call Dr. LaMonte to come check on both of them.

John had refused, but Ralph told him it was an order; he didn't need a wounded employee when there was more work to do. John had accepted, knowing this would be his last and final contact with Ralph. Seemed things were getting heavier every year, and he needed to focus more on the jewelry store business.

Fran paced as she watched the kitchen clock, knowing Salvatore would be home soon, and she had to break the news to him. Knowing how he felt about all of this, he'd surely blame her for all this trouble.

She phoned the hospital to check on Pam and spoke to Elena. "I want you to know I'm so sorry for what happened to your friend. All I can think of is that it could have been you today."

"Well, it wasn't. It was Pam. My best friend."

"As soon as your father gets home, he can follow me down to the university to get your car, assuming the police have concluded their investigation, then we can come and pick you up."

"Don't bother, I'm going home with Ruth tonight. And by the way, two police officers are here now, and I have spoken to them about what I saw when I found Pam. They had already been to the parking garage to check the surroundings and had taken some evidence, as they had told me. They also told me that the car can be moved at any time now. Please give my love to Dad. "

Fran went silent. "Okay, hon. Now don't you worry, just stay with Ruth and call me when you can."

The sound of the garage door going up meant Salvatore was home. Fran put on a pot of coffee, knowing they'd both need the caffeine.

Salvatore didn't take the news well. He blamed his wife and knew she had been meddling; she was mostly responsible for Pam's attack. "We both know this could have been Elena, and how do we know this type of thing won't happen again? We can't take that chance!" Salvatore pushed his second cup of coffee away.

"It won't, I'll make sure of it," Fran said, shaking her head all the while staring at the phone. She couldn't tell her husband what Lamberto had done and what his future plans were. There was enough to digest for the night.

Elena and Ruth had returned from the cafeteria and inquired about Pam's condition at the front desk. The nurse said they would be moving Pam to a private room for the night and added that Pam was asking for her mother. She also said now that Pam was feeling better, the police would be returning within the hour to question her. The nurse had given Elena a note regarding a phone call that she received from Tony Marinetti. He was on his way to the hospital and would be there soon.

Elena looked at the note and took a seat. *He can't come here now! I mean, what if his father was involved in this, and with the police being here soon?*

Ruth informed her that she was going to go back to be with her daughter, and as soon as they had her situated in a private room, Elena could visit her, which would be after the police had finished with their questioning.

Elena was glad to hear the news, but on edge knowing Tony was on his way. If the police had any evidence that connected his father and his buddies to this attack, they'd take Tony and surely interrogate him. But there was no way to call him. She had to take her chances. But in the back of her mind, knowing all that her mother told her about Tony's family and the revenge they wanted, she started to put the pieces together. She couldn't afford for anyone else to be hurt, be it her, her parents, or Tony.

Chapter 24

After Dr. LaMonte had patched up John and Max, Ralph escorted the doctor to the door. "Thank you for coming. You know how grateful I am for your services." He reached out his hand to shake the doctor's.

"Listen, those two were lucky. It's all surface wounds, and Max has a slightly broken nose and some bruises that will take some time to heal. I told him I'll see him in my office tomorrow. And don't worry about the services, you pay me well as it is."

"Thanks, Doc. And maybe Max's big schnoz will look better after it's fixed," Ralph joked.

Ralph walked into the lounge to find John sitting up with a few stitches in his forehead, and Max's nose had a large piece of gauze covering most of the bridge.

"What the hell happened? You both were carrying? I mean —"

"Look, boss, it happened so fast. That fucker Lamberto got me before I knew what happened," John said, reaching for a glass of water.

Ralph took a seat in the overstuffed wing-back chair across from the guys, his dark, beady eyes staring straight at them. "Look, you both know this means war now. We will do away with Elena and those scumbags that were responsible for this."

Max rubbed at his nose. "Don't worry, Boss; we won't screw up next time."

"We'll meet here next week, and by that time, you both will be ready to get back in action. Now go get some rest," Ralph said as he stood and straightened out his grey lounging pants with both hands.

Elena had just walked over to the trash can to dump out her paper coffee cup when Tony came through the entrance doors. She held his gaze, and by the look in his vacant eyes, the news he was about to share with her was not good. He smoothed his hair back with his hand and put his arm around Elena's waist. "Let's talk."

Ruth had gone back to sit with Pam. Elena led Tony to two chairs in the corner of the waiting room, her heart thumping in her ears.

Tony cleared his throat and scanned the waiting room. "Look, Elena, I don't know how to say I'm sorry in a thousand ways, but I can't believe this has happened."

"Tell me one thing: did your father's men have anything to do with this?"

Tony shook his head, searching for words. "I've questioned him, and he denies having any responsibility in this, but I don't believe him. Lord knows I want to, but I just —"

"You just what?" Elena asked as her body shook.

"I just know my father liked you and can't understand any of this."

"One thing I do understand is that this was meant for me, and Pam had to be an innocent victim. I can't deal with this now. And now I have to relive all this when the police get here again."

Tony's face lost all color when he heard the word, police. And Elena knew why. He stood and told Elena he couldn't face them either, whether his father was involved or not; they'd pin it on him or his father. He took hold of Elena's hand. "Look, I'm going to sort this whole thing out. I told Dad I was moving out with you. We can, but I need to follow this thing through first. I love you, Elena, and I promise you we will be together soon."

Elena watched Tony make a mad dash for the doors. She knew he wanted to leave before the police showed up.

As soon as Tony left, two police officers walked in and headed to the reception desk. One was an older balding man, and his partner was middle-aged and well-built. Elena watched them, knowing they'd want to talk to Pam, that was if she was well enough. Elena had already spoken to two different policemen earlier; she wondered why they would question her again or send a different pair of officers. Was it to see if her story remained the same?

The older, balding man turned to look at her as the receptionist must have informed them that Pam would not be having a conversation with them at this time. She knew it would be her — again.

The two officers approached her, and Elena stood. The older officer held his hand out and introduced himself as Officer Ramos and his partner, Officer Henderson.

The older officer spoke first. "I'm sorry to hear about your friend Pam. We know you are already upset, and I'm not here to upset you further, but I do need some information from you."

Elena swallowed hard and nodded her head, "Of course."

Elena's eyes glazed over as she watched both officers pull chairs right across from where she was sitting. *Damn it! Why do I feel as though I'm being interrogated? What if they ask me questions about Tony or his dad? I know I can't lie. And what if I'm implicated? I mean, I've been with Tony these past two weeks. Do I need to speak to a lawyer first?* Her entire body was trembling.

Officer Ramos asked her if she knew anyone who would want to hurt Pam and where they were this morning.

Elena had told them everything that occurred in the university parking garage, and Officer Ramos had concurred that her information had matched that of the medics who took in Pam.

He asked her where they usually hung out and with whom, and whether anyone had reason to attack Pam. He also inquired about a possible boyfriend. Elena knew her friend wasn't seeing anyone.

Elena had told him about the small group of girls she knew from the university, but didn't mention Tony.

Officer Henderson had a small notepad and was taking notes. He didn't have any questions, nor did he look up from his notepad.

Ruth had emerged into the lobby and announced that Pam would be able to answer a few questions now.

Elena ran to hug Ruth. "Oh, this is good news. Can I see Pam as well?"

Ruth looked at the officers.

Officer Ramos replied that Elena could see her friend after they finished questioning Pam.

Ruth led the two officers through the large double doors and took a seat in the corner of the small room.

Elena prayed a lot and thanked God that Pam was alright. Then she wondered if Pam would tell the officers about her relationship with Tony. What did it matter now? The only thing that really mattered was that Pam was going to be okay, but for her and Tony, she wasn't so sure.

Elena paced the lobby, waiting for the police to leave, knowing she could see Pam and make sure she was doing as well as they said she was.

When the officers returned, they stopped to tell Elena they were done talking to Pam, but had just a few more questions for her.

She felt dizzy and had to sit down again.

Officer Henderson went to get her some water as Officer Ramos instructed her to take deep breaths. He sat beside her and waited until she had taken some sips of water and was feeling better before he continued to question her.

Her color was starting to come back to her face, and the dizziness had subsided. She was ready for what she knew was coming, or so she thought.

"So, Elena, I hear you have been keeping company with Tony Marinetti?"

"Yes ... yes, but only for a few weeks."

"Have you met any other members of his family?"

"No, no, I mean ... yes, I have met his father."

"Ralph Marinetti, you mean?" Officer Ramos said, tracking her facial movements carefully.

"Yes, it was Ralph."

"I'm sure you're aware of his affiliation with the mob here in Youngstown?"

Elena had to think about this one, and she'd answer exactly what she knew. "I've heard rumors but have not seen him involved in any crimes, nor his son. And what does this have to do with Tony?"

"Well, we have reason to believe they or their faction may have been involved in this. We are still looking into the disappearance of Dominic Teruzza."

"And you think that was a mob involvement?"

"We are still following all leads."

Officer Ramos put his hand on Elena's shoulder, "Just to let you know, we will be in touch as we may have further questions. Now I hope you have a ride home and get some rest. You've been through a lot today."

Elena nodded but had no words. Yes, it was a lot — too much to handle for one day, and maybe what was to come in the near future.

The door to Pam's room was cracked open as Elena gingerly peeked through, softly greeting her friend. "Hey, lady, good to see you looking better." She walked over to the side of the bed to hug her friend.

"It's good to see you, too." Pam scooted to the side of the bed closer to Elena.

Ruth had whispered to Elena that she was going to return to the waiting room and leave her to talk in private.

Pam looked at Elena with weary eyes, "I ... I'm sorry about the information I gave to the police, but they were insistent and prodding me for every detail. I was so worried you'd be upset with me."

"Look, you don't have to explain. You needed to tell the truth. And how could I ever be upset with my bestie? Come on now. The only thing I need you to do is rest up and get better."

"The doctor says I'll be released in the morning. They have hydrated me and flushed out the drug with the IV.

Hearing the word "drug," Elena shook her head. "I'm so sorry, Pam. This wouldn't have happened if we weren't together."

"What do you mean?"

"I believe that what happened to you was meant for me. You were an innocent victim."

Pam's eyes welled up with tears. "So, who did this to me?"

Elena swallowed hard and had to think carefully before she spoke. "I'm not sure, but I believe it may have been one of Tony's father's men."

"This isn't good, Elena. I mean, you cannot put yourself in danger anymore. Your mother was right about that family."

Elena was about to tell Pam that Tony had visited the hospital when a nurse came in to take her vitals, and Elena knew this was not the time. She gave her friend another hug and walked back out to the waiting room. She wasn't ready to go home again and had planned on spending the night with Ruth at her house.

As Elena entered the lobby, she spotted Ruth talking to Mr. Ramone. And by the look on Ruth's face, she knew something was not right.

Chapter 25

Elena treaded slowly over to where Ruth and her husband were sitting. Paul Ramone, seeing her approaching, did not hide the fact that he was angry. He looked tired and had a five o'clock shadow. Elena sat next to Ruth and reported that the nurse had entered Pam's room to check her vitals.

Mr. Ramone was quick to relay his pent-up feelings. "You know, Elena, my daughter would not be in this situation if not for your involvement with this gangster!"

Ruth took his hand, trying to calm him down. "Now, Paul, we don't have any real evidence that this was related to Tony's family."

"I ... I don't know what to say. You know I would never do anything to put Pam in danger. I'm so sorry," Elena said, shaking her head.

"Well, it's too late for sorry. This can't go on. I've been discussing this with Ruth here, and we cannot let you stay at the house any longer. It's much too risky," Paul shot back. "you'll need to go home or find another place to stay."

Ruth took Elena's hand, "I'm sorry, dear, but he's right. And you need to look out for yourself. You need to go home and be with your family."

Elena turned away with tears filling her eyes. She felt more than uncomfortable now with what was said. She excused herself and walked to the reception desk to use the phone to call her mother.

Her mother informed her she'd be there within half an hour with Salvatore. Elena got up the courage to walk over to the Ramones to inform them of her plans. She also asked if she could say goodbye to Pam.

With their approval, Elena made a short visit to Pam, informing her that her mother was coming to pick her up, but Pam was confused as to why she was not going back to stay at her house.

Elena didn't want to get into the discussion she had just had with her folks, and simply said she thought it was time to spend some time at her own home.

As Elena reached the door, Pam softly called to her, "I love you. I'll see you as soon as I get discharged, and we'll be back to hanging out again."

Elena smiled and blew her a kiss, not wanting to upset her friend and now knowing there would be boundaries set in place with the recent incident, and she had reasoned that it was for the best for both of them.

Fran was getting ready to leave to pick up Elena when Lamberto called. She knew Salvatore was upstairs getting dressed, so she was free to talk.

He first inquired about Pam, and Fran had told him that Elena was going to come home. After hearing this, he asked her how she wanted to take care of things, to make sure Elena was now safe. He himself was ready to end this battle between the two families at no cost.

Fran didn't have to search for words; she knew what she wanted. "Take out Ralph, but don't hurt Tony."

Lamberto didn't disagree with her orders. In fact, he was ready even before his cousin had given him the word. "I'll call Rocky Amato and have him get in touch with my contacts up in Cleveland. It'll be done by the best and with no traces linked to anyone in the family."

There was no need to know the details, just that her daughter was going to be safe as well as the rest of the family.

Lamberto said she'd know when the job was done; he wouldn't need to call.

Elena knew she had better wait outside for her folks, knowing damn well Pam's parents were in no mood to see her mother.

Seeing her parents' Buick LeSabre pull up was a welcome sight, as well as her dad at the wheel. She opened the back door and slid in, expecting another unsettling lecture from her mother. But there was only relief in their comments. Her father was in his usual cheerful mood, and her mother talked about how happy she was that she was finally coming home.

Elena knew this would be short-lived once tomorrow came, and her mother would fall back into her usual dominating role with her "I told you so" attitude. But for tonight, all she wanted to do was have a cup of tea, a hot shower, and climb into bed.

She pulled the top drawer open on her nightstand, pulling out the gold bracelet Tony gave her. She slipped it on her slender wrist, pulled the covers over her, and drifted off to sleep.

<h1 style="text-align:center;">Chapter 26</h1>

Tony knew where he needed to go to get answers. There was one man he trusted, and that was Ross. He was like a second father to him, always there for him. It was Ross who picked him up from school every day and even attended school functions when his father could not. The sad truth was that he knew why.

He headed up Market Street to confront Ross at his home, even though it was 11 p.m. He had to have answers. He pulled up to the modest ranch-style home with simple landscaping, such a stark contrast to the opulent mansion he was raised in. He rapped gently on the door, hoping Ross would hear him. He lived alone and knew there were no others to wake at this ungodly hour.

A weary Ross answered the door wearing a silk bathrobe.

"How the hell did you know it's me? You're taking chances, Ross."

"I peeked out the window and saw the Mustang in the driveway."

Noticing Tony's anxiety, Ross ushered him in and led him into the small living room, where they sat on an overstuffed green sofa.

"What's wrong, Tony? You don't usually visit me this late." Ross held Tony's gaze.

"I need to know the truth. About Elena's friend, Pam, I need to know if you were involved in her attempted kidnapping or knew who was." Tony spoke breathlessly, awaiting a response from Ross.

Ross sighed and waited before he spoke. "You know I walked out on your father the other day. You were there."

Tony nodded, still waiting for what he came for.

"That was the day I knew I couldn't do this any longer. I know how much you care for Elena. I didn't want to disappoint your father. I pretended to go along with his plan, knowing all along I could never do this."

"So, my father wanted you to do the job?"

"Yes, that is the sad truth. Lord knows I've committed many other sins just to serve your father. I know he's been good to me through the years, but I'm too old now to deal with all of this, let alone being involved in a murder."

Tony glared at Ross, "So what was the plan here?"

"I was supposed to accompany Max to the university and inject Elena with an injection of Midazolam. Once she was under, we were to drive her to Lake Erie and dump the body."

Tony shook his head as tears welled in his eyes. "It's absolutely unbelievable. I hate my father!"

Ross patted Tony on the back. "I know it's hard to take, son, but it was his way of protecting you from her family."

"Protect me! What the hell? It was pure revenge, I tell you! Attempted murder!" Tony rose from the sofa.

Ross rose as well. "I'm so sorry, Tony, I really am."

"Thank you, Ross. I knew he was involved, but I had to hear it from you.

And what about this Dominic Terruzza? Was he responsible for him as well?

"Yes, Tony, he was, but I was not on that assignment."

Tony headed toward the door.

"Where are you going now? I hope you don't do anything you'll regret."

"I'm headed home for the last time. I'll deal with my father."

"Promise me you'll keep in touch." Ross put his hand on Tony's shoulder.

Tony nodded and headed out the door, ready to drive home and confront his father. As Tony reached the huge iron gates and punched in the code, he waited for the gates to swing open, allowing him to drive up to the front entrance. He didn't plan on staying, so there was no need to park in the garage. He reached into the glove box for his gun and slipped it into the back pocket of his jeans.

Entering the front door, he could see a dim light coming from his dad's office. His father sometimes kept the desk lamp on in case he had to do business during the night. Tony knew Martin was asleep and Miss Ginny had gone home for the evening. He padded down the hall and heard his father's voice. He waited outside the doorway to listen to detect if there were any other voices.

All he could hear was his father on the phone and his responses, "Yes, thank you for letting me know. I figured he'd go to see him. And if Ross has confided in Tony, then we need to take care of him as well. I'll be getting back to you. Ciao."

So, he had me followed to Ross's house. Fuck him! I need to get to Ross right after I speak to Dad.

Tony entered the office with a purpose. He strode right up to his father's desk, his mouth clamped shut in a tight line. He sat in the high-back chair across from the desk and waited for his father to speak first.

"It's good to see you home, son. How about we have a late nightcap?"

Tony rose from his chair, "How about you tell me why you tried to murder Elena?"

"Now Tony, I don't know where you —"

"Don't fuck with me! I suspected you all along and just got the confirmation from Ross. You are nothing but scum! You're not even a good don, but a scum one!"

Tony had his hand on his back pocket, ready to pull out his Ruger, when his dad walked around to meet him face to face. "Look, I tell you

I had nothing to do with your girlfriend. I like her. She's good for you, makes you happy."

Tony had no words. His father's lies were only fueling his fire. He pushed away from his father. "Don't touch me!"

Hearing shouting, Martin came running into the office, witnessing Tony and his dad in a heated argument. He came up from behind Tony and could see the bulge in his pocket with the handle of the Ruger peeking out.

"Tony! Stop!" Martin yelled.

Tony whirled around to find Martin approaching him with his arm out, ready to retrieve the gun from Tony's pocket. "Ralph, he's got a gun!" Martin shouted.

Ralph leaned against his desk. "Tony, what is wrong with you? You came to murder your father?"

Tony ordered Martin to leave the room. "This is between my dad and me."

Martin had his hand up. "Please, Tony, think about what you're doing. You don't mean to do this."

Tony sat back down, took his hand off the gun, and held his head in his hands.

Ralph had asked Martin to leave them alone; he would take care of the situation.

As Martin left the office, Ralph took a seat behind his desk. He knew not to try to touch his son again. He wasn't ready for more accusations. He spoke in a soft tone, hoping to reason with his son.

"Look, from what I know, Elena is fine, and her friend is fine. I want you to be happy. I'll buy you and Elena a new home, and you can live together. You don't have to do any more dealings for me or have any part of the business."

Tony raised his head. "I *will* be with Elena, and I'll be happy, but not as long as I'm anywhere near you!" I'm leaving tonight, and you'll never see me again. As far as I'm concerned, you're no longer my father!"

Ralph watched his son storm out of the office, his arms by his side, his fists clenched. Martin was right there in the hallway following him. "Tony, please don't do this. You know it will kill him."

Tony turned at the foot of the staircase, "That would be the best thing that could happen to him."

"Where are you going?" Martin was at his back.

"I'm going up to my room to pack, and then I'll leave. And feel free to take anything you want that I leave behind. It may compensate for all the crap you've put up with from my dad over the years."

Martin returned to Ralph's office to find his boss hanging up the phone. He turned to Martin. "I need you to get the Town Car ready for me."

"Where are you going?"

"I'm going to go after Tony. I can't let him leave like this!"

"The car is parked outside in the side lot, sir. I had a private company come by earlier this evening to detail it," Martin said, pulling the tie on his robe tighter. "This new company was cheaper than the other detailers we'd used in the past."

"Well, cheaper don't mean better, but thank you for taking care of the car. Don't bother pulling it around. I'll wait until Tony's left, then follow him. You go back to bed. You've had enough drama for the day," Ralph said as he walked out of the office and headed toward his master bedroom, which was on the first floor.

Martin watched his boss walk away. He turned around and saw Tony coming down the stairs carrying a large black leather suitcase. He walked up to Tony before he opened the door. "I'm sorry, Tony. I know your father loves you and you love him. I think you both can work this out."

"This isn't love, Martin. I know what love is, and this ain't it."

Martin stood as Tony closed the door behind him, shaking his head. *May God help them both.*

Tony headed up Market Street. He was speeding but didn't care. He figured if he got picked up by the cops, he'd mostly get off as his father had connections to most of the local police. It was late. He was headed to

Rock Solid. He had no intention of buying jewelry but needed to get into the basement. He had a key, a key he never wanted, but agreed to do his dad's dirty work for the past few years. But that would end tonight, and if Max Tussi or John Carino were there, he wasn't sure how far things would go.

As Tony pulled into the parking lot of the shop, he could see that Max's car wasn't there, and neither was John's. Things were mostly dark except for the illuminated sign and a small light coming from the back of the shop that led to the office. Tony pulled the Mustang around the back and looked in his rearview mirror before he exited the car. He had the feeling someone was following him, but since Ross had quit, it was highly unlikely.

He grabbed his gun from his glove box and a flashlight and walked toward the back door. He opened the back door and quickly punched in the numbers to the black box on the wall to shut off the security system.

His flashlight illuminated the few desks and dusty file cabinets, but he aimed it toward the door to the side, the one that led to the basement. It was where the dirty files were, the ones he wanted to destroy — ones that had documented all the illegal transactions he had done for his father. He was ready to descend the stairs when his thoughts turned to Elena. It was late, but he knew he had to talk to her. He walked to the first desk to use the black phone that sat atop a stack of papers.

Elena jolted up in bed as her phone on the nightstand rang. She was glad to hear Tony's voice. "Hey, babe, hope I didn't wake you."

Elena quickly came out of her sleepy mode. "No ... no, I was just tossing and turning. Thinking of all that's gone on. Where are you?"

"I'm okay, just at a friend's place. I wanted to tell you to get your things ready by tomorrow evening. We're going away — far away."

Elena whispered, not wanting to wake her parents. "Wh ... Where are we going?"

"Just trust me. As I said, I have a place. Just get your things together, Elena. If I don't leave tomorrow, I'll have hell to pay. I love you and want you to come with me."

"Is it that apartment you talked about up in Cleveland?"

Silence came from the other end of the phone. "Tony?"

"Yes, I'm here. I gotta go, but I'll pick you up at Pam's."

"No, not at Pam's, it won't work. I can't go over there anymore."

"Where shall I pick you up?"

Elena had to think and think fast before one of her parents came into the room. "You know the place."

"Okay. You mean Lanterman's Mill? I know you love that place."

"Yes."

"I'll see you there at 6. I'll meet you in the parking lot. That should give you plenty of time to get your things together."

"See you then. Be safe, Tony."

Just after hearing her words, Tony heard a car pulling up. "I gotta go. love you, Elena."

"Love you, too."

Elena set the phone back in its cradle and looked at her closed door. *I can't believe mom or dad didn't hear the phone? And why did I tell him to be safe?*

She tossed and turned, not falling asleep until after 2 a.m. Tomorrow would be a day that would change her life forever.

Tony heard a car door slam and turned off his flashlight. He had his gun ready as he stood flat against the wall next to the door. He listened for voices but heard none. *Whoever this bastard is, he's most likely been sent by my father. He's going down. I'm done with this bullshit!*

A voice came loud, and it was a voice he knew. It was Max ... Max Tussi.

"Tony! Tony! Please let me in!"

"I'll let you in, alright, but you won't live to leave!" Tony shouted.

"Tony, please! It's your father!"

"Yeah, I know about him. What's he done now?"

"Listen to me, Tony. Your father is dead!"

"Wh-what? What are you talking about?"

"Let me in, Tony. I have to tell you," Max begged breathless.

"How do I know this isn't a trick?" Tony asked, his heart beating fast.

"It's true, I can't believe it myself. I was just going to the house to drop off a late-night deposit, and before I reached the corner, I saw the flames."

"Okay, I'll let you in, but if this is some kind of a joke, you won't be laughing when you're dead."

Tony opened the door, instructing Max to hold his hands in the air as Tony gave him a body pat down. He found no weapons on Max.

Both men stood by the first green metal desk. Max put a hand on Tony's shoulder, "Sit down, son, please, and set the gun down."

Tony held his gaze. "You're serious."

Tony sat, and Max pulled up a folding chair to sit across from him. "As I said, I was just approaching your house when I heard the blast, then saw flames in the air. I knew it was coming from your driveway. I parked my car and ran to your house. Martin was out on the lawn screaming. I ran to the yard to see that the entire car was engulfed in flames. I told Martin to go into the house and call the fire department. I wanted to pull his body out, but I knew it was too late. Too late."

"So, you're telling me you just stood there watching him burn! You piece of shit!"

"I heard sirens and ran. What more could I do? I knew the cops would come, and then after that, the FBI. You know I'm involved in things as much as your father is."

"And involved in the act of trying to kill my girlfriend as well. I heard it all from Ross," Tony confessed. "You're lower than a lab rat!" Tony picked up the gun and, with a shaky hand, aimed it at Max's forehead. "For all the years my father kept you, taught you the business, and this is how you repay him? Running like a pussy? My girlfriend was almost killed, and now you let my father die?"

"No! Tony, you don't want to do this. Think about it. You have the rest of your life to live with Elena. You need to go and see what happened and who was responsible for this!"

"I think I know who's responsible for this, you fucking piece of shit! I can figure it out." Tony still had the gun pointed at Max's head. "You! You went along with his schemes even though you knew it was wrong! You're just as much to blame for what happened."

Max took a few steps toward Tony, but Tony pushed him back. "Don't come any closer. I'm warning you!"

"Go now. Go home to see what they have done with your father. The ambulances and police are most likely still there. It's your duty, Tony."

Tony needed Max to leave, as he knew the cops and the FBI would most likely arrive at the shop soon. They knew he had ties to the mob as well as his father and would most likely tear this place apart.

Tony walked to the door with tears in his eyes, but turned before he opened the door, his gun still pointed at Max. "I think it's fair you go down as well, Tussi." And with that, Tony fired a single shot at Max's head, a kill shot, not even waiting to see him fall to the ground.

He threw the gun on the passenger seat of the Mustang and peeled out of the parking lot, not sure of where he was headed but knowing those sirens would be coming for him soon.

He drove north on Market Street, barely able to see with the tears that had welled up in his eyes. "Dad! Why? Why?"

He headed to Ross's house. He had to talk to Ross before he made his final decision.

Chapter 27

Elena turned over to notice her digital clock read 9 a.m. She never slept this late. She reasoned it must have been the call from Tony last night. She realized she wouldn't make her first class, but she wouldn't make any more of them now that she was running away with Tony.

She rose quickly out of bed, knowing she had a list of things to do in just one day. Her head was spinning. All sorts of thoughts ran through her head. The first one was how she would tell her folks, or even if she would tell them?

Throwing on her robe, she padded down the stairs into the kitchen. Her mom and dad had already left for work, but the coffeemaker was still plugged in with a note beside the machine along with a set of keys — her mother's keys. She shook her head and read the note.

> *Elena,*
>
> *I thought you might want to wait until we had your car cleaned and the window replaced before you drove it. Dad drove me to work today, so you can take mine to school. Your father and I talked about taking you out to dinner tonight at the Train Station for the fish fry. I know it's your favorite. I'll see you around 5.*
>
> *Love,*
> *Mom*

The police had gone over her car and done extensive fingerprint checks before releasing it to her mother. Elena had thought about asking her mother for her car today, but now she didn't have to. Her thoughts turned to Pam, and that scene at the hospital last night kept playing in her head. Was she barred now from seeing her best friend? She knew Pam wouldn't make classes today. She most likely would need some bed rest once she got home.

Then her thoughts turned to her mother and the note. *Well, if she thinks things can simply go back to normal, she's crazy. I'll play her game long enough until I hear from Tony, and then I'm outta here*, she thought as she poured herself a cup of coffee and scoped out the refrigerator for something to eat.

Elena looked at the wall phone and wanted to call Tony, but she didn't exactly know where he was. What she did remember was the tension in his voice. She'd hoped he'd call her soon. The plan was to meet at Lanterman's Mill today. She needed to hear his voice. But she also wanted to call the hospital and make sure Pam was going to be released today. She figured if she called Pam's house, her parents would surely hang up on her.

She dialed the hospital's main number. The receptionist answered. "Yes, Pam Ramone is being released this morning." She informed her that she couldn't be connected to the room as the doctors were now with her, going over the release papers. This was music to Elena's ears. At least her day wouldn't be filled with total dread.

Elena scarfed down a piece of toast and a banana and headed upstairs to get dressed. She turned on the radio in her room and listened to the weather report. Hearing the forecast for warm temperatures and a sunny day, she pulled on her denim shorts and a T-shirt for the first time this year. But all the sunshine in the world wouldn't replace being with Tony. But that would come this afternoon when she'd be meeting him at Mill Creek Park, and their plans would be solidified for their escape.

She focused on packing her clothes and toiletries. She glanced at her art case in her closet that held all her art supplies. She decided to leave that behind. For who knew what would await her with a new life with Tony.

Ross walked down the hall, peeking into the living room, where he saw Tony still asleep on the sofa. He didn't get much sleep last night. After letting Tony in the early hours of the morning, he knew something had happened, but seeing the condition he was in last night, he escorted him to the sofa, handed him a blanket and pillow, and said they'd talk in the morning.

Not wanting to wake him, Ross went into the kitchen and made some coffee. He glanced at the large yellow clock on the wall and saw it was 9 a.m. He tried phoning Ralph, but it just rang and went to his private voicemail machine. He decided to phone Max, knowing his ex-partner would be awake; he always was a morning person. He let it ring several times, but it went to voicemail on his machine as well. Then he remembered Max had a car phone. He tried that number, but no answer came.

He left a message letting Max know Tony was with him and said to call as soon as he got the chance. He poured himself a cup of coffee and just as he put the cup to his lips, Tony had rounded the corner, standing there in his rumpled t-shirt and jeans, his eyes vacant. He looked gaunt.

Ross rose to put a hand on Tony's shoulder. "Sit, son. Let me get you a cup of coffee."

Tony sat, and his shoulders hung low. He needed to confess what he'd done to Max, and release his grief to someone who would understand — someone who he could trust, and that was Ross.

"Look, Tony, I'm not going to pump you for information. Whatever happened, we can work it out," Ross said as he pulled a chair next to Tony.

Tony looked up at Ross with tears in his eyes. "This ... this can't be fixed. Dad is dead."

Ross was at a loss for words. He hung his head so low it hit the kitchen table.

"It was his car — he was blown up in his car," Tony was able to mumble out.

"How do you know, I mean, when?"

Tony took in a deep breath, "Last night, Max came to tell me at the jewelry store. He was on his way to the house and saw it happen."

Ross rose and went to the wall phone again, trying Max's number, but still no answer. He left another voice message.

Tony grabbed the phone out of Ross's hand. "It's no use, he won't — can't — answer. He's dead."

Chapter 28

Tony wiped his eyes and asked Ross to have a seat. His body was still shaking.

Ross gripped his shoulder. "Take a breath, and when you're ready to tell me, I'm here for you." Ross slicked his stringy black hair back with his hand.

"I told you; Dad was blown up in his car last night, and Max just stood there and let it happen."

Ross listened intently, trying to keep his calm as he wanted Tony to remain calm as well, but knew that would be highly unlikely.

"Do you think Max may have been involved — may have been working with another family?"

"Not sure, but I will find out what happened, you can count on that!" Tony stood now pacing the kitchen.

Ross stood and walked to the refrigerator to get a glass of cold water for Tony, but Tony refused to drink or sit down.

"So, don't you want to know what happened to that rat, Max?" Tony's bloodshot eyes narrowed.

"Yes, I do, but I want you to take a few more deep breaths and sit. I'm worried about you."

Tony finally took a seat on the Early American chair and took a few sips of water, slamming the glass down on the table. "Okay, he came to his shop and wanted me to come with him to see what happened to my father, but I thought it was a setup. I mean, I still don't know. He kept coming closer to me, and I felt threatened. I was beyond angry. I blamed him for not rescuing Dad. And he tried to murder Elena! My temper got the best of me and I —"

"You shot him, I get it." Ross took Tony by the hand. "Look, we can figure this out. You have me. You sure he's dead?"

"I'm pretty sure. I didn't go back to check, but I do know how to do a good kill shot to the head."

Ross took in a deep breath and nodded.

"Well, what's our plan?" Tony asked, searching Ross's eyes for an answer. "And Dad knew you were the one who spilled the details about the job he wanted you to do — the job to kill Elena. You need to watch your back as well."

"I can take care of myself, Tony. Let's get you settled. I'm going to call Jack Berone in Cleveland and arrange a place for you to stay. He owes me a favor — a few of them. You need to get away as soon as possible. You and I both know the cops will be here in no time."

Tony froze, hearing Ross's words. He had an ache in his heart and his stomach. He wanted to run back to his house and find out what happened to his father, but he knew that wasn't an option — he was a killer now. A killer just like his father.

His eyes followed Ross as he picked up the wall phone and spoke to Jack. He drank the rest of his water, feeling parched. *Only a mobster would pick up a call this early in the morning,* he thought.

Ross ended the call and took a seat next to Tony. "It's all set. You need to head to Cleveland now. You should be there in an hour. Jack says he'll meet you at LaVetta's Italian Deli in the back parking lot. He has a rental condo just down the street from the deli. It won't be open this early, so he will be there with keys, cash, and other essentials you'll need to hide out for a while."

Tony rose to hug Ross, and he held on tight. His tears trickled down, wetting Ross's sleep shirt. "I can't thank you enough. But when will I hear from you again? I need to know about Dad."

"Don't worry, son. Let me take care of that. I'll be in touch in a day or two. The only thing you have to worry about now is getting out of here. And leave the gun with me. I'll take care of that too. Now go get your things together, you're on borrowed time here."

Tony knew there was one thing he had to do before he left. He had to call Elena, but had to think about choosing his words carefully. He was supposed to meet her this afternoon in Mill Creek Park.

Elena was up early, getting ready to pack another light suitcase, when her bedside phone rang. Her heart leaped with excitement when she heard Tony's voice.

"Elena ... I-I have to tell you something."

Hearing the somber tone in Tony's voice, Elena's excitement was quickly squelched. "What's wrong, Tony?"

"I-I have to leave town. Plans have changed."

"What's going on?"

"It's very bad, Elena. Dad is dead. His car was bombed last night."

Silence came from Elena's end. "What? Who would do this?"

"I'm not sure, but I'll find out. For now, I have to leave. It may be some time before I can come and get you, but I want you to know I love you, Elena."

"I love you too, Tony, and I'm so sorry to hear about your father. But I don't understand — why are you leaving?"

"It's complicated."

"So, when will I hear from you?" Elena waited with bated breath on the other end of the line.

"Don't know. I have to go now. Please stay safe."

Elena put her hand on her stomach and felt an ache deep inside. Her eyes welled with tears. She sat on the edge of her bed, trying to reason what or why this was all happening.

Suddenly, a dark thought invaded her brain — *was it her mother's family? Why?*

Heat rushed through her, and it was as if her entire body was on fire. She marched downstairs, knowing her mother was still home. Her father had already left for work.

She stormed into the kitchen to find her mother pouring coffee into her thermos.

Fran noticed the crazed look in her daughter's eyes. "What's wrong, Elena?"

"Tony's dad has been killed! Murdered! His car was bombed!"

"Wh-what?" Fran set her thermos down and reached out to hug her daughter.

"Don't you touch me!" Elena backed away.

"Tell me your family had nothing to do with this — tell me!" Elena screamed.

Fran's eyes began to water as well. "Sit, please. We will talk. Let me call work and tell them I'll be a bit late."

Elena sat feeling dizzy. She was breathing too hard. Her mother had given her a glass of water and encouraged her to drink. Coffee was not what she needed now.

Fran took a seat at the table across from Elena and reached out her hand to touch her daughter. "Just breathe. Drink some more water, then we will talk," she said, all the while holding her daughter's gaze.

Color began to come back in Elena's face, and her erratic breathing slowed. She waited for her mother to tell her all that she knew about Ralph Marinetti's death.

"I'm shocked! I knew nothing about this. Trust me, Elena. This is terrible news. I'm so sorry."

"Now Tony said he's leaving town and doesn't know when he'll be back," Elena used her hand to wipe the tears falling down her cheeks.

Fran took hold of her daughter's hand, knowing she was hurting. "I know you love him, and he apparently loves you, but I'm going to tell you something you need to hear."

Elena looked up at her mom with concern. "Is this a confession?"

"That morning Pam was attacked, it was Lamberto who saved her. He was following you and was there at the right time and place. Max Tussi and John Carino were the guys who tried to kill Pam, thinking it was you. They had orders to kill you."

Elena accepted a wad of tissues from her mother while she continued to speak. "I will say this again, there is a curse on that family and one that goes back for generations. I knew this, and this is why I wanted you to stay clear of Tony and his family."

"A curse … a real curse," Elena replied. "I don't believe in curses."

"Well, you better believe it. The Marinetti family was involved and is still involved in so many crimes back in Sicily and in this town. It goes way back. And that gold bracelet he gave you — you need to bury it. It will bring you nothing but bad luck. Most likely it's a hot item from one of the many jewelry stores Ralph runs in this town."

Elena thought about Rock Solid and where Tony had spent most of his time. She wondered if her gift was truly a stolen item and if what her mother was saying was true.

She rubbed her wrist where she had put on the bracelet last night before bed. "But what about your family? We know Lamberto and a few of your cousins are no saints." Elena glared at her mom.

"You are correct, but we had to protect ourselves because the Marinettis tried to take over my parents' butcher shop years ago in Italy. Your grandparents!"

Elena's eyes got as big as saucers. "But that's no reason to become killers. I know about Lamberto and his 'hit man' title."

Fran took a deep breath. "I won't deny it, and I will stand by my family and condone their actions. I will do anything to protect you. Now, as far as Tony goes, I'm so sorry for his loss, and he will need time to get over this. You can't let this ruin your life."

Elena stood and walked to the kitchen window, looking out at her mother's statue of the Virgin Mary and the small shrine that surrounded it. "For the devout Catholic you are, I still can't accept the fact that you and your family would ever get involved with crime."

She walked behind her daughter and put a hand on her shoulder. "I've never lost my faith, dear, and I continue to pray for you and Tony. He's in danger, and you are too as long as you continue your relationship with him."

Seeing Elena holding onto the kitchen counter, Fran realized her daughter needed some food in her stomach. "Sit and I'll make you a bagel and cream cheese. You need to eat."

She made sure Elena ate before gathering up her purse and thermos and heading out the door, but then came right back into the house with the morning edition of the Youngstown Press. She laid it on the table for Elena to see.

The headlines read:

Ralph Marinetti, Youngstown's Biggest Mobster, Killed Last Night in a Car Bombing

Chapter 29

Elena waited until her mother left to call Pam so she could speak to her in private. She guessed she'd still be at home, recovering. If there was one person whom she could lean on, it was Pam. As her shaky fingers dialed the numbers, she prayed Ruth wouldn't answer; she'd most likely hang up on Elena or make an excuse to not let Elena talk to Pam. But she got lucky; Pam answered on the second ring.

"How are you doing, my friend?"

"I'm much better, and I miss you. I really wanted to go to class today and see you, but the doctor and my folks thought it would be better if I rested a few more days."

"That's wise. School can wait. In fact, I didn't go either. "Elena took a few deep breaths before she was ready to hit Pam with the news. "There's something I need to tell you."

"What's wrong? Are you okay?" Pam's voice was riddled with alarm.

Elena searched for words. "No ... not really. There's been a terrible accident."

"Who?"

"Tony's dad was killed in a car bombing last night. Did you see the headlines in the paper?"

"No. I'm still in bed. Dear Lord! I'm so sorry! Who did it? "

"I ... don't know, but Tony called me early this morning and said he had to leave town today."

"Really? Why would he do that when his dad was just killed?"

Silence came from Elena's end. "I'm not sure. It's all so odd."

"Did he say when he'd call you?"

"He didn't know. His voice was so sad, and I hated to ask more questions, considering what happened. Today was the day we were supposed to meet."

"I know. I'm sure he'll call you when he can. He's most likely too upset."

"I'm just glad you're safe. This whole thing has gotten crazy. I mean, with the attack on you and now Tony's dad — I don't know if any of us are safe anymore. I'm scared for both of our families and us as well. "

No answer came, but Elena could hear Pam's television on in the background.

"Oh no!" Pam shouted.

"What's wrong?"

"I've got the news on, and a breaking report just came in. A Max Tussi was found dead at the Rock Solid jewelry store early this morning. He was one of the owners. Where have I heard that name before?"

Elena felt dizzy and had to sit down. Earlier, she had wanted to tell Pam he was one of the men who tried to kidnap her, but had decided to wait until Pam was fully recovered. She had just learned this information herself this morning.

She had to respond. "I believe he was a friend of Tony's dad."

Elena's nerves were on edge, and she knew she had to end the call fast. She promised to call Pam tomorrow and told her that since she couldn't visit her at home, she'd see her at the university later in the week or at the coffee shop, unless she left with Tony.

Elena sat down at the table. She tried to understand what had just occurred. *Did Tony have something to do with this? Why would he suddenly have to leave town? Did he kill Max? But why would he?*

Then it suddenly dawned on her — he might have found out that Max was the one who tried to kill Pam and had been ordered to kill her!

It was too much for her to handle. She decided to skip her afternoon classes today and try to find some answers. But how? She didn't know where Tony was, but she did know where her mother was. She quickly pulled on some jeans and a t-shirt and headed to Step into Style, the boutique her mom worked at. She would confront her right there.

Tony was just pulling off the interstate after meeting with Jack Berone when he heard the radio station broadcast the news about the death of Max Tussi. He took his eyes off the road, and the car veered to the right, almost hitting the guard rail. He knew the police would find the body sooner or later.

He steadied himself and the car, sped off the exit, and headed toward the Parkman Condo complex, where Jack had given him a key to one of the condos. He thought about his short meeting with the middle-aged man who was dressed as though he were attending a funeral. All dark clothes, huge, wide-brimmed hat, and dark glasses. *Guess he wanted to be incognito*, Tony reasoned. The man didn't say much, only handed him the key and said he'd be in touch.

He pulled into a large parking lot facing rows of grey and white stacked condos. He found the space numbered 102, where Jack told him to park. Pulling a baseball cap down over his head, he grabbed his suitcase and headed toward the condo, praying no one would recognize him. It wouldn't be long before his photo was plastered all over the news and in the papers as well.

He entered the condo and saw it was modestly furnished but with newer furniture. In a sitting area, there was an overstuffed gold sofa and two white wingback chairs across from the sofa. A small oak café table took up most of the small kitchen area, and there was a bar with two tall barstools. He carried his suitcase into the bedroom where a queen-size bed sat under a small window, flanked by two nightstands with tall bronze lamps. He headed into the kitchen, wondering if there was anything in the refrigerator.

He shook his head in appreciation when he saw the assortment of fruit, meats, and cheeses. *Thank you, Ross and Jack.*

He looked at the small console television and felt no desire to turn it on. Pouring himself a glass of water and fixing a light snack, he sat at the bar planning his next move.

Elena pulled into the parking lot of the small boutique and headed into the shop. Her mother gave her a quizzical look when she saw her come through the door. She was helping a customer with some dresses. She excused herself and met Elena at the register. "What are you doing here? Aren't you supposed to be in class?"

"Max Tussi has been found dead!" Elena blurted out, her hands on her hips.

Fran looked at her daughter with surprise. "What?"

"Don't play games with me, Mother. I'm sure you know who he is. And possibly you had your killer cousin take him out!"

"Please lower your voice, Elena. You're scaring the customers."

"Scaring the customers? Let's talk about being scared, shall we?" Elena glared at her mother.

"Let's go outside. You're upset."

Fran looked around to see if anyone was within earshot. "I can honestly say that neither Lamberto nor any of his friends had anything to do with this. This is all news to me. But you need to remember that if not for Lamberto, your friend would be dead by now."

"I-I want to believe you, but everything is so unbelievable right now. I just don't know who to believe. I mean, who would do this?"

Fran put her hand on Elena's shoulder. "Have you wondered if Tony could be the killer? Or was it possibly a random robbery? It was a jewelry store, after all."

"No! No! Tony would never do such a thing. I mean, he was upset over the attack on Pam, but I don't think he'd kill Max."

"Why don't you wait around for a bit. I have a break coming up, and we can go to lunch?" her mother offered.

"I don't feel like eating. I'm going home. I'll see you after work."

Elena peeled out of the parking lot, her mother still standing by the shop's door watching her. *Something is off. I've got to call Lamberto and see what's happened. I know if anyone knows what's happened, it would be him.*

Fran waited until the shop was empty, then called Lamberto. She almost hung up before he finally answered.

"Hey, what's up?"

"I need you to level with me. Did you have anything to do with Max Tussi's death?"

"First of all, we shouldn't be having this conversation on a public line, but no, it came as a shock to me as well. I just heard the news myself. I'm going to call Rocky Amato and see if he's heard anything. When I know anything, I'll call you at home. As you and I both know, Ralph had numerous enemies in this town."

Fran ended the call and, with not much appetite herself, decided to skip lunch so she could leave work earlier that day. Her daughter was distraught, and with all that had gone down lately, she worried about her own safety. Maybe it was time to have Lamberto spend more time following Elena until this whole thing cleared up.

Chapter 30

Elena walked into an empty house. She glanced at the wallpaper in the kitchen, a pattern of roosters and flowers that was long overdue for an upgrade. She wondered why, if her mother's family had any mob money stashed away somewhere, they hadn't moved from their modest home to a nicer one.

Her thoughts turned to her dad. He would be home in a few hours. She missed him. He was always the positive one in the family and the one who believed in her. She was certain his family never had any ties to the mob. There were a lot of good Italian families that had no affiliation with these crime families.

Just as she was about to go upstairs to her room to take a nap, the phone rang. Her heart jumped, hoping it was Tony. To her surprise, it was Ross. He kept the call short, asking if she'd meet him somewhere as he had something to tell her. She asked him repeatedly if he knew where Tony was, but he told her they'd talk at an unpopulated place. One place came to mind for Elena, and that was Lanterman's Mill. Ross agreed. They set a date for the following day.

After the call ended, Elena couldn't help but wonder what information Ross would divulge to her. She knew he meant the world to Tony. His name had come up during many of their conversations.

It was nearing dinner time, and Elena's stomach was rumbling. She rummaged through the cupboards and fridge. She found three zucchinis and some mozzarella cheese. She opened the vegetable bin, hoping to find some tomatoes. And with luck, she found two large beefsteak tomatoes. She knew how to make a zucchini lasagna and set to work. She figured it would take her mind off things if that was at all possible.

While the lasagna was baking, she thought she'd catch up on her class projects. She'd missed a few classes and still didn't know if Tony would call, and they'd be leaving soon. The plan was for her to finish her classes in Cleveland. But all of this was quite uncertain now. She pulled out her sketchbook and added some details to the sketch she'd recently done.

Her dad walked through the door with a big smile on his face. He was home earlier than usual. His dark hair was sticking up in all sorts of directions, mostly due to the dust and sweat at the warehouse. "Now that's how I like to see my girl — at home and working on what she loves."

Elena rose to hug her dad.

"Mmm, something smells good. Did you cook?"

"Yes, I made zucchini lasagna. I figured it would help take my mind off everything that happened yesterday."

He put his hand on Elena's shoulder. "Yes, I know. That's why I'm home early. I heard the latest about Tony's dad and his friend Max. I'm so sorry. I'm sorry for Tony."

Elena began to cry. Her dad hugged her again, reassuring her all would be fine, but deep inside, he wondered if his wife's cousin was involved in one or both of these crimes.

Salvatore sat down with Elena as they waited for Fran to come home. "You know, my dear, we've had many crimes involving the mob here in Youngstown. Usually, after a big fatality like this, most of those who were involved will be put away, and others will hide out. Tony will be questioned, and I wouldn't be surprised if you will be as well. Just like you were questioned after Pam's attack."

Elena hadn't thought about that possibility. She was far too busy wondering if Tony was okay. Now her thoughts shifted. *What do I have to hide? Do I have to talk about having sex with Tony? And what about Mom? Lamberto? Would the police or the FBI come to the house?*

When she smelled the lasagna in the oven, Elena quickly came out of her trance and jumped up from the table. She took out the large casserole dish and placed it on a cooling rack.

Elena kept her secret meeting with Ross from her dad, and she'd surely keep it from her mother, too. She looked at the wall clock and noticed that her mother should have been home an hour ago.

Salvatore excused himself to take a shower and said they'd all wait for Fran to sit down and have dinner together.

* * *

Fran had decided to make a quick pit stop at Lamberto's, hoping he'd be home. She knew she couldn't call him on the phone at home. She was on edge ever since Elena showed up at the shop today.

Ever since the death of his wife, Lamberto was rarely home. The house reminded him of his wife too much with all the homey touches she'd done. Fran pulled into the driveway behind Lamberto's Cutlass Supreme.

He quickly ushered her into the modest living room. He offered her a beverage, but she replied she was there for a reason and had no time for a social visit.

Lamberto took a seat across from Fran in an outdated leather chair. "So, to tell you the truth, I've not heard any news about Max's death from my connections. And none of my guys were involved."

"But you took care of the Marinetti issue, did you not?" Fran tilted her head to the side, waiting for the answer she wanted.

"Yes, cousin, it was taken care of. And rest assured, there will be no trace of me, you, or anyone else in the family. The Donatos and Russos remain clean."

"That's good to hear. Now I want to ask you another favor," Fran stood to look out the living room window, her hands on her hips. "I want you to follow Elena for a few weeks."

"That won't be an issue. She's family, and I want her to be safe as well."

With those words, she hugged Lamberto and headed out the door. She stopped when she noticed a white van parked across the street and turned to inform Lamberto, her eyes full of worry.

"Oh, their son is in a rock band, and that's their van," Lamberto replied, aware of her concern.

Fran nodded, breathing easier, "Guess I'm just being paranoid."

"It's okay, cuz. We all need to be these days, but as I said, leave it all to me."

Fran pulled onto the highway heading home, still glancing in her rearview mirror now and then.

Chapter 31

The smell of garlic hit Fran's nose as she entered the kitchen. "You made dinner?"

"Yes, I had to do something to take my mind off everything," Elena said, taking a sheet pan of garlic rolls out of the oven and placing it on a cooling rack.

"I was getting worried about you, Fran. Just about to call the shop," Salvatore said as he set another plate down on the table.

"Sorry, I'm late, just had a short meeting with the boss." Fran set her purse down on the kitchen chair and went over to hug Elena. "It's good to see you home again. You know it's about time this family sat down and had a regular dinner together."

Elena was mostly quiet during dinner. There was no mention of the murders, which she was thankful for, although she noticed her mother picked at her lasagna. She suspected something was going on but didn't want to ask her; she was too occupied with her meeting tomorrow with Ross. Her nerves were so on edge she didn't know how she'd manage to get through her two art classes tomorrow morning.

After a hot shower, Elena felt a bit more relaxed and headed down to the kitchen for a cup of tea. It was a warm night and the window was open. The tulip-printed curtains billowed in the breeze. She could see her mother kneeling out back by the shrine of Our Lady. *She is either praying for forgiveness or praying that I'll stay home for good.*

When the kettle whistled, Elena backed away from the window, not wanting her mother to notice that she was watching her. She took her tea into the living room and sat in the antique rocker that had belonged to her grandmother Russo. She thought about her, wondering how much her grandparents had been involved with the mob. They were both born in Sicily; she was well aware of how many gangsters hailed from that area.

She heard her mother open the kitchen door. She continued to sip her tea until her mother walked into the living room with her rosary beads. "Are you alright?" Elena asked.

"Yes, dear. Just doing my usual nightly prayers. I decided to take advantage of the warm weather and visit the shrine." Fran sat on the sofa, setting her beads on the coffee table. "Mind if I join you?"

"I'd like that. I'll make you a cup of tea," Elena said.

"No, please just relax. You cooked dinner. Let me get it myself."

Elena watched her mother walk out of the room with a bit of a limp. Wearing that old housecoat made her seem as though she'd aged ten years. She reasoned it was mostly due to stress, and stress that was self-inflicted.

Fran came back with a steaming cup and set it on a coaster on the coffee table, letting it cool.

Salvatore came downstairs after his shower, hearing their voices. He refused Fran's offer of a cup of tea, knowing they needed some mother-daughter time. He bid them goodnight and headed off to bed.

As soon as her dad was out of earshot, Elena had to ask the question that had been bothering her for some time. "Just how far back does your family go with this mob stuff?"

Shocked by her daughter's question, Fran took a deep breath. "I can tell you only what I know. Grandpa Russo met some men when he came to Youngstown to work in the steel mills. I remember him coming home and telling us we would soon move into a bigger house and wouldn't have to worry about money anymore. He came home later and later after work and would be gone for days sometimes, saying he had work out of town. I knew my mom was suspicious as I overheard many conversations between her and her sister. I was smart, just like you."

"So did he get involved with the other crime families here?" Elena asked.

"Only one, and that was the Marinetti family. It went back to when they lived in Sicily. They pretty much took our butcher shop business away from us. Took a fifty percent cut. Threatened to kill my family. That's when my mother went to the village Strega to have a curse placed upon them."

Elena's eyes grew wide. "A curse? Grandma went to the village witch? I know what that is!"

Fran nodded her head. "Yes, she thought it was the best thing to do at the time. But the old woman had told her that her powers were getting weaker and warned her that the curse she had placed might not hold strong enough to weaken the Marinetti's strong hold over the village."

"So, the Marinettis come from the same village in Sicily? You'd think you would all get along."

"On the contrary. They only grew bigger, taking in more families who had gone along with their schemes, only hoping to get richer, believing the lies the Marinettis told them. Fools! The crime family continued to grow when they moved to the States. Seems as though the curse never worked."

"I'm not superstitious, and I don't believe in those old curses. And, by the way, Lamberto is old. Why is he still involved in this?" Elena asked.

"It's not a choice. We still need to keep our guard up. Look how they took out Dominic Terruza, Lamberto's friend!"

"You're sure it was Tony's father's men who did this?"

"Without a doubt. Never found the body. Never will."

Fran took the last sip of tea and set her cup down. "It's late. We both need to get some sleep. And one last thing, remember what I told you about that bracelet?"

Elena shook her head, not wanting to start another conversation or bring up the fact that she would be leaving with Tony as soon as she heard from him. She could tell her mother was tired, and there would be a better time to discuss this.

Chapter 32

Elena had a restless night. Thoughts of meeting Ross the following day kept her tossing and turning. What news could he possibly have for her? Good or bad, she'd find out tomorrow. The only thing that brought her comfort was the gold bracelet, which she now wore on her wrist. She loved the feel of the smooth gold band and the engraved letters that represented love.

The sound of her blaring alarm woke her at 7 a.m. She had two classes this morning. As she stumbled out of bed, she remembered she hadn't finished her drawing assignment last night. She was too caught up in the conversation she'd had with her mother.

As it was still early, she quietly descended the stairs and headed to the kitchen for coffee, but stopped at the bottom landing when she over-heard her mother talking with her father. It was Lamberto's name that caught her attention. She stood there wanting to eavesdrop as long as she could.

"I think it's best to have Lamberto follow her to school for the next few weeks," Fran said. "It's most likely this thing will end now that Ralph is dead, but for now we need to be on our toes."

Her father had agreed with her mother; that was a first.

Elena felt a knot in her stomach. *He can't follow me today. I'm meeting Ross! Who knows what he'd do to him? Damn it! But they said he'd follow me to school; maybe he won't follow me to Mill Creek Park? I'll tell them*

I'm going to a study group at the city library, but I need to let Ross know to be on the lookout for "the Lamb."

By the time she entered the kitchen, her folks were finishing breakfast, and her mother had set a cup at the table for her. "Early morning classes?"

"Yes, two of them," Elena said, as she took her cup over to the coffee pot, trying to avoid her mother. Her father gave her a peck on the cheek and told her to enjoy class, then headed out the door.

Fran couldn't help but notice the scowl on Elena's face. "Something wrong, dear?"

Elena turned to face her mother, her brows furrowed. "You know, I don't need your cousin to follow me around anymore. I'm a grown woman and can take care of myself."

Fran looked at her with surprise. "Who said —"

"I heard you telling Dad just now."

"It's simply a safety precaution, Elena."

"Safety precaution?"

"Did you already forget that you were targeted for murder just last week? But it was your friend who was attacked instead?"

"No, I haven't, but I'm sick of all of this. And maybe you should know now that I'm planning to leave with Tony as soon as he gives me word that all is ready," Elena said in a commanding tone, wanting her mother to know how she felt.

Fran stood with her mouth agape. She watched Elena fill her coffee and head upstairs.

Elena slammed her bedroom door and hurried to get dressed. She waited for her mother to come knocking on her door, but there was nothing. All she heard was the garage door open, which meant she was leaving for work.

As she picked up her art kit and headed out the door, she looked at the phone. *How could she reach Ross without having his number?* She thought about calling Lamberto to tell him off, but decided not to, figuring that it would only make things worse.

Having rushed out of the house without breakfast, she pulled into the Coffee Corner shop to order a bagel with cream cheese and a coffee to go. She scanned the parking lot as she exited with her breakfast in hand. No sign of Lamberto yet.

Pulling into the parking deck, Elena had thoughts of the day Pam was attacked. She hadn't seen her friend in a week and missed her. *Would there be another attempt, and would whoever did it get it right this time?* Dizzying thoughts swarmed her head. She grabbed her art kit and backpack and swiftly headed to her first class with her unfinished assignment.

She had an hour break between classes and headed over to the library in hopes of catching Pam, knowing she had the same break and usually spent it at the library. The library was empty, with only a few tables filled with some members of the football team. *Hmm, first time I've seen them in here studying,* she thought. But no sign of Pam. She reasoned she would have time to phone her before she met Ross. She'd also hoped Pam's father had time to cool off and would let her visit her at her house.

Her second-period art class dragged on. Professor Elmore's lecture on the French Renaissance just about put her to sleep until Sean Dutton, a dark-haired young man sitting across the table from her, handed her a note. It came as a surprise; they barely spoke outside of class, though they had partnered up a few times for an assignment. He was an attractive guy with dark brown hair that hung to his shoulders. He reminded her of the singer Todd Rundgren and thought he was attractive, but since meeting Tony, she'd paid no mind to him.

Making sure Professor Elmore was not looking her way, she read Sean's note:

> I'd like to meet you for coffee sometime to chat about
> the upcoming art show.

Elena quickly folded the note and placed it in her purse as Sean watched, waiting for a reaction. She gave him a big smile but didn't reply to his note.

She checked the cafeteria again; still no sign of Pam. Elena's heart raced, fearful that something bad had happened to her again. She rushed out to the parking lot, searching all the rows of cars, unable to find Pam's. *I'm sure she will be back in class now. I mean, it's been a week. What could have happened?*

She arrived home around 1 p.m. and couldn't wait to call Pam. But the call went to the answering machine. *Something must be wrong!* Elena's heart thumped as she jumped in her car and headed over to Pam's house.

Turning the corner, Elena could see a white sign in Pam's yard.

FOR SALE
Booker Real Estate
330-1276-2245

Pam's car was in the driveway. Elena pulled in, hoping to find her friend and learn what was going on.

Ruth answered the door and greeted her coldly. Pam was right behind her mother.

"You guys moving?"

Pam's mother stepped aside as her daughter walked out into the garage to talk with Elena. "Yes, I wanted to call you and tell you. Dad thought it would be best if we got away from this town. I mean ..."

"You mean from me? My family?"

"No, don't take it that way. It's just that after what happened to Tony's dad and me, we can't take any chances."

Elena shook her head. "I-I don't know what to say. I mean, what about your classes?"

"I will enroll at the University of Pittsburgh. Dad's company is letting him get a transfer."

Elena's stomach tightened, and tears pooled in her eyes. "This is sad news, Pam. I mean, we've been friends since elementary school."

Pam ran her hand through her bushy shag and looked away, trying to hide her tears. "Listen, I'm not that far away, and we will always keep in touch. It's only an hour and a half drive. I still love you, my friend. Don't ever forget that."

Elena held on tight to her friend. "How soon are you guys planning to leave?"

Pam stood back, holding her gaze with Elena's. "As soon as next week. Dad's company has already found a place, and the realtor is handling the house sale."

"I wish nothing but the best for you and your family," Elena said, wiping her tear-filled eyes with her hand.

"Well, I gotta run and help mom with the packing. I promise to call you before we leave."

"Promise?" Elena asked, reaching out for her friend's hand.

"Promise."

Chapter 33

As late afternoon approached, Elena readied herself to meet with Ross. With the news of Pam's moving, she needed to hear something good. She fixed herself a snack and took it up to her room. She turned on the television, and several news channels were reporting updates on the investigation into Ralph Marinetti's death, along with Max's.

It was the last reporter who got her attention. He had claimed that Tony Marinetti was a suspect in the death of Max Tussi and was nowhere to be found. The police and the FBI were searching and had received several tips on his whereabouts. She knew it wouldn't be long before she would be investigated. But what could she tell them? She knew nothing of Max's death. She'd tell them the truth, that she had a short relationship with Tony, and that was it.

And where exactly was Tony? She had no recent calls from him. She couldn't call the house, knowing he wasn't there. Hopefully Ross would have some answers for her.

She pulled her long black hair into a ponytail, put on some new jeans, and a red Henley t-shirt. She had an hour and decided to arrive at the park a bit early. Ripping out a paper from her notebook, she left her folks a note telling them she had left to meet the study group again.

Pulling into the parking lot by Lanterman's Mill, she found it was mostly empty. She parked, locked her door, and headed toward the old mill, hoping to enjoy the peaceful sound of the water washing over the mill's wheel and finding a sense of calm, a calm she needed now more than anything.

Hearing a car engine, she glanced toward the parking lot. A black van had pulled into the lot. She stood looking to see who was driving, but it was too far away, and the windows were all tinted so dark. She didn't remember Ross having a van; when he worked for Ralph, he always drove the Town Car.

Who the hell is this? It wasn't Lamberto; she knew he drove a silver Cutlass Supreme. She looked at her watch and saw it was only 4:30. Feeling shaken, she didn't know if it was the FBI, Tony's dad's friends, or Ross using a different car. No one had exited the van. It just remained parked in the lot. Now she wished it were Lamberto. At least he was family.

Not ten minutes later, a black Buick pulled in and parked next to her car. She prayed it was Ross. From her viewpoint, she could see a tall, dark-haired man wearing Ray-Bans exit the car. She stood as Ross saw her and waved. Her breathing relaxed, knowing it was him. He was wearing a suit jacket, which she thought was much too heavy for a warm afternoon. He strode toward her with a smile on his face.

Elena walked over to meet him at the entrance to the mill. He reached out his hand to greet her. "It's good to see you, Elena. Let's walk while we talk," he offered.

"Did you notice the black van in the lot?"

"Yes, and not to worry, it's my cover."

"Cover?"

"Even though I have left my affiliation with Ralph Marinetti, I still need to be careful."

Elena nodded, knowing he was right.

"Got a good place here where we can sit and talk? Ross asked.

Elena suggested they cross the small bridge and walk over to a small pavilion on the other side of the park.

The pavilion was empty. Ross said this would be perfect as he sat across from her at the picnic table. He removed his shades, revealing striking hazel eyes, but ones that seemed to convey sadness.

Elena took a deep breath and asked what she had been most worried about. "Where is Tony?"

"Tony wanted me to come here personally and talk to you."

Elena's heart pounded, waiting for some reassuring words from Ross.

"He's gone into hiding for a while. He needs to do this for his own safety and yours, for that matter."

"Hiding ... where?"

Ross scanned the area once again, making sure no one was around. "He's up in Cleveland staying at a friend's place. He's okay."

"He … uhh ... wants me to tell you that he may be gone for a while."

Elena shook her head, tears welling up in her eyes. "Why couldn't he take me with him? I don't —"

"I know, Elena. But why would he put you in danger? The police and the FBI are on his tail."

"Why on earth would they think he murdered his own father?"

"He didn't, but he was involved in another murder."

Elena shot up from the bench. "No! Tell me he didn't kill Max!"

"I'm afraid he did. Said he had to have revenge for his father and what he did to Pam."

Elena paced back and forth. "I'm trying to wrap my head around this. So Max was the one who bombed his dad's car?"

"We don't know. Tony does know that Max stood as the car burned, then ran. He could have pulled Tony's dad out."

Elena sat back down, feeling weak. "This is too much. I don't know if I can deal with all this. Have the police and the FBI questioned you?"

"Yes, they have, and they found no reason to believe I'd kill Ralph or my longtime partner, Max. But they know I know people, and they will be poking around for some time. I'm going to protect Tony at all costs; that's why I stopped working for Ralph. Too many crimes. But they can't pin these last two murders on me."

"But what about Tony? He may get caught and go to prison!"

"Not to worry about that. He's got his dad's connections, and they will do as much as they can." Ross stood and walked around to sit beside Elena. "Now, lastly, he wanted me to tell you to stay with your family. You will be protected."

Elena gazed up at him quizzically. "By whom? Lamberto?"

Ross nodded. Yes, I know Lamberto. Partly, but there are others. Once this case is solved, this chapter should come to an end. Ralph's men will move on to another crime syndicate, break free here."

Ross noticed a black Cadillac pull into the lot. Not recognizing the owners, he reached inside his suit jacket, revealing a holster that contained a gun. Elena watched him. "You're carrying?"

"Yes, I am." He kept his eyes on the Cadillac. No one emerged. "Listen, Elena, we need to leave soon."

Ross walked Elena to her car, never taking his eyes off the Cadillac and with one hand on his Colt 38.

"Will you please tell Tony I love him and to get in touch with me when he can?"

"Yes, I promise," Ross said, making sure Elena was seated as he closed the car door. He waited until her car was well out of sight, then he walked to his car, still watching the Cadillac. No one had gotten out, but he wasn't taking any chances. This wasn't his first rodeo.

Chapter 34

Elena gunned it and made a turn onto Forest Creek Road, noting that the black Cadillac had turned as well and was speeding up behind her. *Where's Lamberto now? Damn it!*

Elena kept looking in the rearview mirror. The Cadillac pulled up beside her, but suddenly Ross's car was on its bumper. The Cadillac jerked to the side, seeming to have a blowout. It was louder than a blowout. Elena knew that sound — it was a gunshot. She didn't look back again in her mirror, but floored it all the way home, struggling to catch her breath.

She could barely keep her eyes on the road as she drove home. So many tears had blurred her vision. All she could think about was Tony and what he was going through. Everything had changed. With shaky hands on the steering wheel, she pulled onto State Road and noticed Ross was still following her. *What the hell?*

Pulling into the driveway, she sat for a moment trying to catch her breath. She knew it was Ross who came to her rescue, but wondered what happened to the Cadillac and who was in it. Laying her head on the steering wheel, she now believed what Ross said about her being in danger.

Fran came running out to the driveway after noticing Elena's car was home, but she hadn't come into the house. Elena looked up at her mom with tears in her eyes.

Helping her daughter out of the car, Fran wrapped her arm around her daughter's waist. "Let's get you inside."

Once inside, Fran led Elena to the living room sofa, where she sat on the edge, sweeping some long hairs out of Elena's face. "What happened?"

"Tony ... he's gone and for a long time!"

"How do you know that?"

"Because I just met Ross and he told me everything," Elena sputtered out between sobs.

Fran shook her head. "You met Ross Vincenzi? Where?"

"Does it matter?"

"I thought you were at a study group."

"No, I met him at Mill Creek Park, and he told me everything that has happened."

"Do you realize how dangerous this was?" Fran shouted, her hands moving up and down.

Elena could only sob.

"Look, you need to tell me everything he told you," Fran said, handing her daughter a wad of tissues. "And let me get you a glass of water."

After a few gulps of water, Elena was ready to talk. She had to tell someone. She wanted to call Pam, but that would only put more fear into her, and she'd most likely never see her again.

Fran listened to every word Elena said. She didn't hold back anything, not even the shots fired at the Cadillac.

Seeing how upset her daughter was, Fran wasn't going to lecture her, but she would make damn sure her daughter was safe.

"I know you're upset. Your father will be home in an hour, and we have to tell him everything as well. There are no secrets in this family."

Elena looked at her mother with anger in her eyes, knowing damn well there had always been secrets. But right now, she needed to get undressed and take a hot shower. She could smell spaghetti sauce coming from the kitchen. It smelled good, but she wondered if her stomach could hold any food down now.

Fran stood up, holding onto Elena's arm, trying to steady her. "Now just take it easy. It's all going to be fine. We are a family and a strong one. You have to have faith, Elena," Fran said as she watched her daughter walk to the stairs.

As soon as Elena was out of earshot, Fran called Lamberto and told him what had happened and asked why he wasn't following Elena.

His excuse was that he'd thought she was just a few streets away at a study group.

With Fran's dire warning that this recent occurrence had upped the ante, he and his Amato friends in Cleveland needed to be on their toes. And not just to watch Elena but herself and her husband as well. After all, she knew Lamberto was responsible for Ralph Marinetti's death.

Elena lay on her bed staring at her phone. *I can't even call Tony or Ross. I feel so helpless. How could Tony send Ross to deliver a message he should have done himself? So now he's a murderer, and who knows when I'll ever get the chance to see him again? This is so fucked up. My friend gets attacked, and now my family's safety is at risk as well.*

Reaching into her nightstand and pulling out the gold bracelet, she examined it closely. *If it's true what my mother says about it bringing bad luck, then I need to get rid of it soon. Maybe Tony had no idea it was a bad luck charm, or someone placed a curse on it from another family, knowing he'd give it to me? Maybe there's a strong Strega in one of the other families?*

Elena heard her mother calling her down to dinner, but she didn't have much of an appetite, even though she loved her mother's Italian spaghetti.

Salvatore was already sitting at the kitchen table. By the sullen look on his face, Elena could tell her mother had informed him of the recent incidents. He stood to give Elena a strong hug.

Fran's attitude was not her usual self; she smiled and told Elena she had made her spaghetti just for her. She acted as though nothing had occurred, and the family was going to have a nice meal tonight.

Elena, turning to her dad, was the first to start the discussion. "So, I take it Mom has filled you in on what happened today?"

"Yes, she has, and I agree with your mother that steps to assure your safety and ours will be set in place, but we will talk about this later. Let's just enjoy this wonderful meal."

Fran, noticing that Elena was picking at her food, changed the subject: "Well, what's your next art project?"

Elena sat for a moment, realizing she had been so upset the past week that she hadn't focused on her artwork. "It's just a landscape drawing."

"Sounds lovely. You need to keep your grades up. I know you want to go for your master's degree someday and teach college art," Fran said, reaching for a second helping of salad.

"Yes, you are so very talented, Elena. I'd like to see that as well," Salvatore chimed in.

Hearing a car door slam, Fran ran to the picture window in the living room. Two policemen were walking toward their porch. With her heart pounding, she ran back into the kitchen. "The police are here!"

Elena rose from her chair. "What do they want?"

There was no time to answer as they heard two loud knocks at the front door.

Salvatore instructed his wife to answer the door and stay calm.

Two uniformed officers from the Youngstown Police Division stood at the door. The older balding man identified himself as Detective Logan, and the other officer, a much younger man with a bushy mustache and long sideburns, introduced himself as Officer Wagner. They asked to speak with Elena Donato.

Fran introduced herself as well as Salvatore and called for Elena, who was still sitting in the kitchen.

Elena rounded the corner, her face white as a sheet. She had expected to see the same officers who came to the hospital, but these were different men.

Fran asked if she and her husband could remain in the room, and the officers said it was fine.

Elena, along with her parents, sat on the sofa. The two officers sat across from them on the Early American wingback chairs.

Officer Logan spoke first. "I just have a few questions regarding the disappearance of Tony Marinetti. We understand you have been seeing this young man."

Elena answered with a simple "Yes."

"Can you tell us the last time you were with him?" Officer Logan asked, holding Elena's gaze.

She had to think for a moment, not wanting to reveal she had been at the hotel with Tony. "I think ... I think it was at his father's house. We had dinner."

Officer Wagner took notes in a small notebook while Officer Logan asked her a few more questions.

"Have you had any recent calls from Tony or from any contacts associated with him?"

Elena froze. She looked to her mother, noticing a stern look on her face and knowing exactly how her mother wanted her to respond. But she already knew how she would respond. She would never reveal Tony's whereabouts or the fact that she had met up with Ross Vincenzi. "No, I've had no calls or contact with him."

Elena shivered inside, knowing she had just lied to the police and would be held accountable for her actions.

"Well, we believe he may have been involved in the murder of Max Tussi," Officer Logan said as he looked to his partner, who was still taking notes. "Please contact us should you hear anything from him."

Elena nodded while Salvatore spoke up, "Are there any further questions, officers? As you can see, my daughter has been traumatized by these entire events. Her best friend was attacked, as you probably know."

Officer Logan nodded. "Yes, we are aware of the entire situation. So, this is all we need for now. Elena, make sure you will be available for any further questioning."

"Of course," Elena replied.

The officers thanked Elena and her parents and let themselves out.

After Elena shut the door, her knees grew weak. She headed back to the sofa, her parents by her side. "Look, you have nothing to worry about. You are not a suspect in any of this," Salvatore said, his arm around his daughter.

Elena turned to her mother, "I'm so sorry. I've brought nothing but trouble to my friend and our family. I never asked for this. I never wanted to bring this into our family."

"Listen, Elena, we know this. We are family. We're all going to be fine. Trust me when I say this." Fran placed her hand over Elena's.

Salvatore nodded, standing to excuse himself; he had an early work day tomorrow and wanted to get to bed.

Fran suggested that Elena take a hot bath and also retire early. But Elena had other plans. As soon as her parents were asleep, she was going to Rock Solid, and she would bury the bracelet. If it was cursed, then she needed to return it to where it came from. She thought about it also being the very place Max was killed. *Maybe the place was cursed or on some sort of hallowed ground?* She reasoned Tony most likely didn't even know if it had been. *But did Max? After all, he was a part-owner of the store along with John Carino.* And she wondered about John Carino and what had happened to him.

She knew going there could be risky; the FBI could still be searching the place for clues, but she didn't care. That bracelet was returning home.

After her bath, Elena entered her parents' room, kissing them good night. She returned to her room and threw on a pair of shorts and a long-sleeved shirt. She tucked the bracelet in the pocket of her shorts. It was another warm night for late April.

At midnight, she tiptoed downstairs and into the garage to retrieve a trowel and a small flashlight. She scoped out the street to see if anyone was watching their house before backing up her car and heading onto Youngstown Poland Road and then the freeway. Few cars were out, and she didn't care if she was being followed. She was on a mission.

All was dark at the jewelry store except for the lighted sign and a light at the back entrance. No cars in the lot. No police. No FBI in sight. She parked in the back lot and quickly walked over to a patch of grass bordering the lot. She turned on the flashlight, dug a small hole in the dirt, and placed the bracelet in the hole. "There now. I send you back to the very place you came from, and here you shall stay," she said softly, thinking how smoothly these words rolled off her tongue.

Elena sat in her car for a few moments, thinking about what she had just done. Was it the right thing to do? Was her mother right about the bracelet? She didn't know, but she had to trust it was. She rubbed her right wrist where she had worn the bracelet, wondering if what she had done would mark an end to her and Tony's relationship. What she *did* know was that she still loved him. A dark thought suddenly crossed her mind. She could drive up to Cleveland and look for him. That's where Ross said he was staying, but how would she find him? Hopefully, he'd find her one way or another.

Chapter 35

Sunlight peeked through the blinds in Elena's room as she lazily peeled back the covers. She looked at her clock, realizing she'd slept in until 9 a.m. She sat up in bed, remembering what she had done late last night. It was Friday, and she had only one class later in the day, but she wanted to catch her mother before work. She padded into the kitchen to find her mother getting ready to leave, pouring coffee into her thermos.

"Oh, I hope I didn't wake you," Fran said.

"No ... I wanted to tell you something," Elena said, making eye contact with her mom.

"What's wrong, Elena? Everything okay?" Fran's eyebrows raised.

"Yes, I wanted to tell you I buried the bracelet last night. I thought about everything you said and thought it was for the best."

Fran put her arms around her daughter, tears pooling in her eyes. "I'm sorry. I know how much this hurts. I didn't want it to come to this."

"It's okay, Mom, really. I'm okay."

Elena pulled back, allowing her mother to see a small smile on her face. "As you said, 'It's all going to be okay. Now have a nice day at the shop, and I'll see you at 5.'"

After Elena walked her mother to the door, she poured herself a cup of coffee and went into the living room to sit on the large red recliner.

The morning paper was placed inside the magazine rack. She pulled it out to read the headlines:

Funeral Set for Mob Boss Ralph Marinetti

Elena set down her coffee mug, feeling a pit in her stomach. The service was scheduled at St. Matthew's Church on Tuesday. She read the obituary, which named his surviving family members. Tony's name was listed first, then the aunts, uncles, and cousins. She laid the paper on her lap. *I've got to go. I know Tony will be there. He wouldn't miss his dad's funeral. This is my chance to see him, and hopefully we can finally be together.*

* * *

Drawing class seemed to drag on as Professor Elmore clicked through a slide show of French Renaissance artworks. She was fixated on Ralph's funeral and hopes of seeing Tony there. After class, Sean Dutton stopped her in the hallway, grabbing hold of her arm. "Hey, you never answered my note. What do you say to having a coffee with me today?"

He'd caught her off guard. She accepted his invitation, agreeing to meet in half an hour at the Coffee Station just across from the university. Watching him walk away, she had second thoughts. Then it occurred to her that if the cops *were* following her and they saw her with someone other than Tony, they would think she had a new boyfriend. Meeting Sean would be a good cover.

* * *

Tony heard a knock at the door of the condo. He peered out the window, his Ruger in his hand. It was the delivery boy with his groceries. He opened the door, accepting the two large bags from the scrawny young man and handing him a tip. He carried them over and set them down on the bar. *Thank God for Ross. Ross! I have to call him about Dad's funeral.*

Tony knew Ross would try to talk him out of going, but there's no way in hell he'd miss it. Besides, he needed to find out what happened when he spoke with Elena.

Ross had just gotten off the phone when Tony called. "I take it you know better than to attend your dad's funeral," Ross said.

"You know that's not going to happen. I need to be there."

"The Feds are still looking for you. You can't take that chance — you know they'll be there. Even if you came in the best disguise, Tony, they would know it's you. You'd be a sitting duck. They've got fingerprints and all the evidence on you now. You can't risk this," Ross said, his voice authoritative.

"Tell me about Elena."

"She misses you. She's hoping to see you. She wants to hear from you, but you and I know the best thing is to stay away from her."

"It's been hard not seeing her, but I get it. I almost called her the other day, but my gut told me not to."

"I believe they've tapped her phone and will trace that call. Don't even think about it."

There was silence from the other end.

"Tony, let's get real. I'm going to tell you what you need to do."

More silence from Tony's end.

"You with me?" Ross asked.

"Yes, tell me what you have planned."

"I can get you a ticket to Italy, a small village called Pacentro. You have some distant relatives there who will take care of you."

"Italy, huh?"

"Italy. This small village is in a remote part of the Abruzzo region. Not much happens there."

"So, I just give up my life to go hide out in some ancient village with no life like some damn hermit?"

"It's either that or you go to prison for murder."

Tony sat down on the small vinyl barstool, thinking about what Ross said. "Okay, if I go, then I want to take Elena with me. You can make that happen, Ross. It's the only way I'm going."

"I'm not sure how this will play out, but I'll look into it. What if she doesn't want to go? You just had me deliver a message to her that indicated you want her to get on with her life. And I'm not getting involved in a kidnapping."

"She'll want to go, Ross, believe me. I want her to go. I need her."

"Let me make some calls, and I'll get back to you. Don't do anything stupid, Tony."

"I'd call her myself, but I can't if her phone is being tapped."

After ending the call, Tony reached into one of the grocery bags, pulled out an apple, and took a bite. Discovering it wasn't the kind of apple he liked, he flung it at the wall.

Ross phoned Jack Berone to see if his contacts would be able to charter a plane and get passports within the next few days. Every step he made to help Tony implicated him more deeply, but he felt he owed it to Tony, knowing the kind of pain he was in now.

Chapter 36

Elena looked through her closet for the perfect black dress to wear to the funeral. She grabbed a short black baby doll dress off the hanger and held it up to herself as she looked in her dresser mirror. *It's perfect. Now I need a headscarf as well.*

She rummaged through her mother's drawers, knowing she had several scarves—ones she wore over her head to church. A sheer black one with tiny sparkles in the fabric was just the right one.

Her mother met her as she was walking out of the bedroom. "Where are you going?"

Caught off guard, Elena couldn't think of a response fast enough. Besides, she knew the look on her face gave her away. "I'm going to Tony's dad's funeral."

Fran shook her head, taking her daughter's hand. "That would be a very stupid move, Elena. You seemed resolved to the fact that this relationship is dangerous, and now you want to rile things back up again?"

Elena took in a deep sigh. "I want to see Tony. I know he'll be there."

"Well, I doubt he will. He'd be a fool to show up. The Feds are looking for him. Don't take this risk, Elena."

Elena went into her bedroom, shutting the door. Fran stood outside trying to compose herself. She didn't want to get into another confrontation with her daughter. All she could do was let her go and have Lamberto tail her.

Elena was about to head out when the phone rang. Her heart leapt, hoping it was Tony.

It was Ross. Elena's stomach lurched, wondering why he was calling her again. He'd told her to meet him right away at Belucci's Market; it was urgent.

Elena grabbed her jacket and drove like the wind up to the market, not even checking to see if she was being followed.

Ross was seated in his parked car, and she pulled next to him. She got out of her car and entered the passenger side of the Buick.

Ross made it clear he had just a few moments to talk. When Elena heard what Tony wanted her to do, she just about lost her breath. "How can I go to Italy with him? I mean —"

"I can have all the details sorted and a plane ready in a few days."

"But, what will I tell my family?"

"Tell them the truth. You don't need to lie and have the Feds on your tail as well, let alone worry your parents to death."

"I ... I don't know what to say. Can I think about this?"

"Not much time, Elena. He has to get out of the country soon. His time is running out."

"I'm going to Ralph's funeral. I know Tony will be there. Maybe I can talk to him."

"I've warned him not to attend and hope he heeds my message. And you need to stay clear of this as well. I'll call you on the day of the funeral, and you'll need to let me know your decision. You are the only one who can decide this."

"Will you be there?"

"No, I will not. Shortly after I make arrangements for Tony and you, I'm leaving the state."

Elena promised she'd have a decision by Sunday.

After she left the parking lot, she knew there was one person she needed to talk to, and that was Pam.

Looking at her watch, she realized she had missed her class, but given her conversation with Ross, none of her classes seemed to matter at this point.

She headed to a phone booth on the corner. She took a chance at calling Pam and got lucky.

"I was just thinking of you and going to call. I've got some news for you," Pam said in a sombre tone.

"Yeah?

"Yes, we are moving next week. I wanted to meet up with you before then."

Elena was sad to hear about the move but looked forward to seeing her bestie. She knew she might be out of the country soon, so she asked Pam if they could meet tomorrow. She remembered what her mother had told her about their phone being tapped. She needed to let Pam know what was going on.

"Can you meet me tomorrow around noon at the Coffee Corner shop?"

"Perfect. See ya then."

Ross called Tony, informing him of his conversation with Elena. He also warned Tony to stay put, but Tony had other plans. There was one question he had to ask Ross. "I know you've done so much over the years to help me, and I will never forget it. I need you to find Dad's killer. If anyone can, I know that you can find him."

"Tony, I quit working for your father shortly before he was killed. I have had enough of this business, but I'll do this one thing for you. I'll get in touch with some contacts in Cleveland, but I want you to stay out of this," Ross demanded.

Tony agreed, and Ross promised he'd get back with him when he had any leads.

What Ross didn't tell Tony was that he had heard from a trusted contact and already knew who was involved. He would confirm it before telling Tony, but knew it would break his heart.

What Tony didn't tell Ross was that he'd secured a rental car and one of Jack Berone's men had delivered a black suit to the condo. He'd planned on lying low until the funeral on Tuesday.

He would have to be well disguised. He had been keeping abreast of the latest updates on the searches for his dad's and Max's killers and knew Youngstown police and the FBI were following some clues.

He would forgo the church service because he didn't want to enter the church carrying a weapon, but he would attend the graveside service. He planned to keep his distance so no one would notice him. If Ross's plans went well, he and Elena would be off to Italy a few days after the funeral.

* * *

Elena sat in a booth next to the window at Coffee Corner, waiting for Pam. She thought about the last time they were there and the two goons that were following them. She scanned the outside lot looking for anything that looked out of the ordinary.

When Pam's Honda pulled in, she rose and waited for her friend to join her.

Wearing bell-bottoms and a green jersey that contrasted nicely with her auburn hair, Pam attracted a few looks from some of the guys sitting at the counter. Elena could tell she'd had a recent cut as her shag was shorter and layered.

"You look great!" Elena rose to hug her friend.

It didn't take long for Pam to notice the dark circles under Elena's eyes. "You okay?"

Elena suggested they place their orders, then she'd tell Pam what was happening once the waitress was out of earshot.

"So, what's going on, Elena? I know you missed me, but something tells me there's more to it than this."

As soon as the older blonde waitress had delivered their drinks, Elena was ready to drop a bombshell on her friend. First, she glanced around the shop once again to make sure nothing looked suspicious.

"Okay, you're killing me!" Pam said.

Elena laid out all that Ross had told her. Pam, in near-shock at what she was hearing, didn't interrupt until Elena was finished with the mind-blowing announcement.

"You really going through with this?"

Elena nodded. "Yes, I am, but I do want to know what you think about it."

Pam reached for her friend's hand. "Look, you know I love you and want you to be happy, but have you considered what this all entails? I mean, have you even thought about what it would do to your parents?"

"I have. But I'm not leaving without telling them, so they don't have the FBI looking for me."

"I get it that you love Tony, but moving to a different country is a whole new life."

The conversation paused when the waitress arrived with their burgers. Between bites, Pam continued to lay out the possible consequences for Elena's decision, including the fact that they may never see each other again.

"But you could come to Italy and visit."

Pam shook her head. "That's a long shot, my friend. I don't know if I would ever travel out of the country."

Finishing their lunch, Pam looked at her watch, indicating she needed to leave soon.

Seeing Pam stand up to leave, Elena realized she had forgotten to tell her about the bracelet.

Pam sat back down and looked at her friend quizzically. "Really? Do you believe in that sort of stuff?"

"I'm not sure, but my mom had me convinced it may have been really cursed," Elena said, reaching for the bill.

"But you loved that bracelet!"

"I can't take any chances, Pam. Too much has gone down way too quickly."

The girls walked out together, Elena leading the way. She told Pam to wait at the door, and she'd signal for her to come out in the lot. Once she saw it looked clear, Elena walked Pam to her car.

"You see what just happened?" Pam said, turning to Elena. "You're still afraid. You need to think about this. You'll be running away with a man wanted for murder. You'll always be on the edge."

Elena nodded. She gave Pam a strong hug and told her she'd call her before she left, if everything went as planned.

"You know, I think about what happened to you just about every day. It was my fault. I'll live with it forever. Maybe my going away will make it safer for everyone."

"Just be sure this is what you want, and as I said, I want you to be happy."

Elena watched Pam drive off. She walked to her car, tears clouding her vision and thoughts of Pam's words filling her head.

Chapter 37

Fran had to call Lamberto to tell him about Elena's plans to attend Ralph Marinetti's funeral. She took a longer lunch break from work and went into the back room where she could talk in private. Lamberto agreed to her request but mentioned that he needed to keep a low profile as the Feds were still investigating Ralph's and Max's deaths. Everyone was still a possible suspect. He'd have to keep a distance while keeping an eye on Elena.

As soon as the call ended, Fran started to have a feeling that something was wrong. She always relied on her intuition, just as her mother did. She called her boss to ask if she could leave early, and getting an ok, she headed home. She hoped she would find Elena there.

Fran breathed easier when she spotted Elena's car in the driveway. She entered the house through the kitchen, calling out for Elena. Getting no response, she headed upstairs and found Elena's door closed. "Elena, it's Mom. Can we talk?"

When Elena opened the door, Fran was shocked to see a large suitcase open on the bed filled with Elena's clothes. "What's going on?"

Elena reached for her mother's hand. "I'm leaving with Tony in a few days. A friend of his is making all the arrangements."

Taking her daughter's hand, she led her to the edge of the bed. "Are you crazy? Do you know if you're caught with him, you'll be accused of being an accomplice!" Her eyes shot daggers into Elena's.

"We don't plan on being caught. I love Tony and want to make a life with him." Elena turned away from her mother and threw another shirt into the suitcase.

Fran stood, her arms flailing in the air, "Look, Elena. I love you, and I want you to think rationally about all this."

"I'm going, Mom, and there's nothing you can do to stop me."

"When do you plan on leaving?"

"After the funeral, Tony and I will leave for Italy."

"ITALY!" Fran shouted. "I was afraid of something like this."

"Nothing to be afraid of, Mom. Tony has men who will protect me until we're out of the country."

Fran felt overwhelmed and didn't know what else to say to Elena. Salvatore would be home from work soon; maybe he could talk some sense into her. After all, Elena did have a closer relationship with her father.

Salvatore knew something was afoot the minute he'd stepped into the kitchen, seeing his wife at the kitchen table with her head in her hands. Dropping his briefcase on the floor, he laid a hand on his wife's shoulder. "What's happened?"

"It's Elena!" Fran cried.

"What? Is she okay?" Salvatore pulled his wife toward him, locking eyes with hers, which were red and swollen.

"She's okay, but it's what she's about to do that's not."

Fran told her husband about Elena's plan. He listened intently, not responding until she was finished. "Let me go upstairs and speak to her. I never imagined she'd do something like this. Don't know what she's thinking."

Salvatore spoke softly behind Elena's closed door. "It's Dad. Please open up."

When Elena opened the door, Salvatore reached for her hand, not missing the almost-filled suitcase on the bed. "Your mother told me of your plans. I'm not here to scold you, but at least hear me out."

Once they were seated on the edge of the bed, Salvatore sighed. "Listen, your mother and I love you more than anything and want you to be happy. But what you're planning is beyond dangerous, and you haven't thought this through."

Her eyes welling up with tears, Elena found the words she needed to say. "I love you too, Dad, but I'm following my heart. I love Tony, and if I don't go, I'll never see him again, and I won't be able to forgive myself."

Salvatore nodded. "Elena, Elena. I myself have made several mistakes in my lifetime and know what it is to live with them."

Elena looked at her father quizzically. "What do you mean?"

"It's a long story, one I don't want to get into now. It's in the past, and I'd like to keep it that way."

"But this is no mistake; I feel it," Elena said.

Salvatore stood to leave the bedroom, "Promise me you'll give yourself some time to think this over before you make a life-changing decision."

Elena didn't reply and remained seated on her bed after her father closed the door on his way out.

Fran was still at the kitchen table when Salvatore came downstairs. Her face lit up with hopes of some good news, but her husband didn't tell her what she wanted to hear. She knew their daughter would not change her mind. He pulled up a chair beside her and shocked her with what he was about to say. "I think you need to call Lamberto."

"I already have."

Salvatore reassured her that everything would be fine as long as Lamberto takes care of things on his end.

* * *

Tony rose early Tuesday morning, filled with anticipation and anxiety. Thoughts of seeing his dad's casket being lowered into the ground made him nauseous, but hopes of Elena being there and ready to head to Italy with him gave him hope. He chugged down a few cups of black coffee, smoked three cigarettes, and got dressed. He slid his Ruger into the slim leather holster under his black suit jacket. He figured he needed to be ready for anything.

* * *

Elena woke to a gloomy morning. Rain was predicted for later that day. Dark clouds loomed overhead as Elena drove to St. Matthew's church in Youngstown. She tried to remember what her grandma used to say about rain at a funeral, something about tears to wash away pain and sin. Italian grandmas were very superstitious, and everything had a meaning.

Fran watched her daughter enter the kitchen wearing the black baby doll dress and carrying the headscarf. "You're going, aren't you?"

"Yes, I am. Even if Tony's not there, this is something I need to do for myself and for Tony." She walked over to the sink where her mother was washing dishes.

Fran wiped her hands on her flowered apron and gave her daughter a strong hug. "Be careful, Elena. I'll see you back home later this afternoon."

She stood at the kitchen window until she heard the door shut, then walked out to the shrine outback, kneeling and asking Our Lady to watch over Elena. Lamberto could only do so much; her strong faith offered more.

Chapter 38

Lamberto had just gotten off the phone with Rocky Amato. Lamberto told him of Elena's plans to run off with Tony, saying it had to be stopped at all costs. Rocky agreed. He said he'd drive down shortly and be at the cemetery for cover.

Lamberto planned to tip off the police. It was the final card he held and he had waited until the last possible moment, hoping he wouldn't have to use it. After ending the call with Rocky, he phoned a longtime buddy at the East End Division of the Youngstown Crime Unit.

The clerk who answered the call took his name and transferred him to Officer Louis Bartell's office. "Been a long time, Lamberto. It's good to hear from you again."

"Yes, but I must make this short. Time is running out. It's a family matter."

Lamberto told Louis that Tony Marinetti might show up at his father's funeral and dropped a few other valuable tidbits of information. "My cousin's daughter will be there, and I want her to be safe. Make sure that happens."

"Yes, we were planning on having our men in the area. We suspected Tony would be at his dad's funeral. What else do you have for me?"

Lamberto divulged Elena's plans to run off with Tony after the funeral.

"I'm ending this call now. Remember our agreement. You make sure she's safe, and I don't just mean during the funeral," Lamberto insisted.

"I know exactly what you mean. I can't risk losing one of my best informants."

Seeing the huge brick church shrouded in dark clouds gave Elena goosebumps. She saw the black hearse parked out front, and her stomach did flip-flops. She didn't know how she could get through this, but she would try in hopes of seeing Tony.

She covered her head with her mother's scarf and headed for the large double wooden doors. The pews were filled, and Mass had already started. She sat in the last row, so she could make a quick exit if she felt sick. If she did leave early, she would wait outside until the service was over, then follow the procession to Greenlawn Cemetery, which was just a few blocks away.

Elena looked around the packed church. *Who were all these people? Can a mobster have that many friends? Where's Tony?*

The priest asked the congregation to pray. Elena took part, her eyes still scanning the rows of pews for Tony. With everyone's backs to her, there was no way she could find him.

It was time for friends and family to approach the casket, which was closed and covered in ruby red roses. It was a closed casket, and Elena reasoned Ralph's body was most likely burned beyond recognition. She hoped now she would get a chance to see Tony's face among the crowd.

A few older ladies with black lace veils covering their faces sobbed at the casket. She'd assumed they were family. They had to be pulled away by two men who were next in line. She noticed Martin and Miss Ginny in the line. Her thoughts shot back to the night she had dinner at the mansion, a happier occasion.

After observing all who had come up, she concluded Tony wasn't here. She couldn't miss his jet-black hair and strong, chiseled features, even in a crowd.

After the service had ended, she made a beeline for the doors. She didn't want to be noticed, as if anyone from his family would notice her. She headed to her car and waited for the cars to form the procession to the cemetery. *Tony has to be there*, she thought as she followed the last car in the procession.

She turned the radio on low, hoping music would settle her nerves. Led Zeppelin's "Stairway To Heaven" was playing, and she thought it was ironic, considering the circumstances. She wondered if Tony would make it to heaven, given the jobs he'd done for his father. But she believed in her heart he would be forgiven, as he claimed he was cutting ties to a past life of crime. His father, however, most likely bought a one-way ticket to hell.

Her eyes scanned the long procession of cars, and there was no sight of Tony's Mustang. She reasoned that he would most likely be in a different vehicle, not wanting to be noticed.

She turned on the windshield wipers as the rain started coming down at a steady pace. The procession arrived at Greenlawn Cemetery, and she waited patiently behind a long line of cars slowly entering through the large black wrought iron gates.

He has to be there. I have to see him. He has to tell me we are going to Italy. The words kept playing over in her head until it was finally her turn to advance up through the entrance.

She followed the cars to the far back side of the cemetery, where they parked along the road. She saw a large angel statue in front of an enormous stone mausoleum. Rows of folding chairs were set up under a white tent. She sat in her car watching the crowd take their seats. From her viewpoint, she could see the casket set up. A different priest walked to the front of the tent and began the prayer service. She grabbed her umbrella and made her way to the area, each step feeling like her feet were made of lead.

She took a seat in the last row, where there were a few empty chairs left, covering her head again with the black scarf. Once again, she couldn't tell if Tony was among the many people dressed in black with their backs facing her. From the back row, it was hard for her to hear what the priest was saying, but she couldn't miss the loud sobs of the many people seated in the tent.

The rain subsided, now reduced to a trickle. She looked behind her, hearing more cars pull up. She wondered if Lamberto was one of them, but didn't see a silver Cutlass. There was a black Buick among them, and she watched as a tall young man wearing a black suit and black Ray-Bans emerged from the car. She knew that man; it was Tony!

Elena froze in her seat. *Should I run up to him or wait until he gets closer?* Her heart raced. *I need to let him do what he came here to do, and that is to pay final respects to his dad.*

Her eyes followed his every move as he walked slowly toward the front of the tent. Most of the people had already thrown a rose onto the casket as it was being prepared to be lowered into the ground.

She stood to get a better view of what was happening in front. No one seemed to recognize Tony. She wondered how this was possible, knowing his relatives were present. Maybe everyone was too involved in their own grief to notice, she conjectured. She wanted to run up and hug him, telling him how sorry she was, but she would wait — wait until he paid his last respects.

Now was the time, the time to go to him. Wiping tears from her eyes with her scarf, she stood and thought about wanting to feel strong, strong enough to give Tony hope. She came up behind him as he knelt next to the casket in prayer.

"I'm sorry, Dad. Sorry that I left you. If I hadn't left, you wouldn't have gotten in that car. Please forgive me."

Elena placed her hand on Tony's right shoulder. He turned around, his eyes filled with tears. "Elena! He died because of me, because I ran out on him!"

"No! No! Don't blame yourself, Tony." She put her arms around him. "I'm here for you and always will be. Ross told me about the plans, and I'm ready to go. I'll go anywhere with you."

Elena locked eyes with Tony, seeing him shake his head. "I ... I can't leave now. I must find his killer."

Tony knelt back down by the casket, which was still lying on the rails. He picked up a small pile of dirt and threw it over the casket. "I'll find them, Dad, I'll find them."

"But it's not safe, Tony!" Elena said, pulling back from him, trying to read his face. He was grieving, and she didn't want to pressure him by pushing any further plans on him. He was in a weak state.

One of the caretakers had indicated to Tony that they were going to lower the casket.

Tony stood up and held Elena's hand. "I'm sorry, Elena, but I don't know when I'll see you again. I need to take care of business first. I can tell you this, though: I love you."

Elena nodded. "I understand. It's what your father would want you to do."

Tony was quiet, eyes still following the casket as it was being lowered into the ground.

Most of the crowd had filtered out, and a stream of cars were departing. Elena saw two black Chevrolet Impalas pull up and park on the side of the road next to another mausoleum. Two men in dark blue suits emerged from one of the cars. They wore silver lanyards around their necks bearing an emblem she immediately recognized — the FBI.

Elena grabbed Tony's arm. "It's the FBI!"

Tony turned and saw the men advancing toward him. He turned to Elena. "Run!"

Elena stayed frozen, right by Tony's side. "I'm not leaving you!"

The taller, middle-aged man strode toward Tony, yelling, "FBI. Stay where you are!"

Tony reached under his suit jacket, where he had his Ruger, but the bald, older FBI agent drew his weapon first. "Drop it, Tony Marinetti. You are under arrest for the murder of Max Tussi!"

The two caretakers had just finished putting the casket in the ground when they looked up to see what was happening.

Tony stood frozen, eyes on fire, ready to engage in a battle when Elena walked in front of the two FBI agents. "Don't shoot! Let him go! Doesn't he have the right to spend a few more moments with his father? For God's sake, this is a burial!"

"If you don't move, lady, you'll be arrested for obstructing justice!" the older man yelled."

Tony softly told Elena to go and leave quickly.

She slowly walked away to the curb, where she witnessed Tony dropping his gun to the ground.

The two agents advanced and handcuffed Tony. "No! Let him go!" Elena called out. A hand touched her shoulder from behind; she turned to find Lamberto standing there.

"What —?"

Lamberto wrapped her in his arms. "It's okay, trust me. He'll get a good lawyer and be out before you know it."

Elena held his gaze, not knowing whether to trust him or not. But for now, she was too shaken up to worry about Lamberto's promise.

She watched Tony walk off with the FBI agents. He didn't look back at her as they put him into one of the black Impalas.

Still sobbing, she let Lamberto walk her to her car after the FBI agents drove off. She didn't see his car, but there was still another black Impala in the lot. Lamberto opened the car door for Elena and told her to go home. Her family was waiting for her.

She started the car. Through her tears, she noticed Lamberto climbing into the other black Impala. *Did he possibly? No ... he wouldn't.* Dark thoughts clouded her mind, but her emotions pushed them aside, and all she could think about was Tony and what would become of him and of them, for that matter.

Chapter 39

Over the next few days, Elena remained in her room, glued to the television for the latest news about Tony's arrest and others involved in the murders of Max Tussi and Ralph Marinetti. The forensics team had found Tony's fingerprints at the jewelry store. She heard Tony had obtained one of the best attorneys in Youngstown, but reports said he would most likely be indicted for first-degree murder.

Fran had brought meals up to Elena's room, begging her to at least get some fresh air or come out to the front porch and sit with her and Salvatore, but her attempts were futile. She was too consumed by what had happened.

She'd gotten a call from Pam, who had heard the news and wanted to meet for lunch on the weekend. Pam's family had already moved into their new house in Pittsburgh. Elena couldn't wait to see her old friend again. She needed someone who understood and with whom she could confide in.

After ending the call, her thoughts returned to the day Pam was attacked, and guilt swept through her once more. It would be a memory that would stay with her forever. She had been so blindly in love with Tony that she had forgotten that her friend had almost been killed if not for Lamberto. Lamberto! Yes, she also wanted to ask her mother if he had gotten a new car, seeing him get into the black car at the cemetery. It was so strange that he'd arrived at the same time as the FBI.

Pam was gracious enough to drive all the way into Youngstown to meet her friend. She knew Elena was still grieving and didn't want her to make the drive.

Elena cried when Pam pulled into the parking lot next to her. It seemed like ages since she saw her friend, but it had only been a short time. They entered the small Italian café and took a booth in the back where they could chat in private.

Pam complimented Elena on her new shag cut, which resembled Pam's but was slightly longer. Elena appreciated her friend's kind words, but she knew damned well how tired she looked. They talked about their classes, and Pam had asked Elena if she had done any more drawings, which she had not. Pam was ready to start her student teaching in the fall and was so excited about it. She mentioned she'd met a guy in her literature class and they already had two dates. Elena perked up and wanted to hear more details.

The conversation turned to Tony. Pam wanted to hold off on the subject as long as possible, but knew her friend wanted to talk about him.

"You know, Pam, I thought I'd be somewhere in Italy by now with Tony, but fate had other plans."

"I guess it did, my friend," Pam said, taking hold of Elena's hand from across the table. Pam waited to ask the most difficult question. "Are you able to visit Tony in prison?"

Elena shook her head, "Not at all. He's in the Denton Correctional Facility, and only close family are allowed. Trust me, I've tried to contact him but to no avail."

"I'm sorry, my friend, but you have your whole life to live, and I truly believe things happen for a reason."

"Now you're sounding like my grandma," Elena produced a small smile and shook her head.

"Guess so."

The girls parted ways in the parking lot, with no fear of being watched or followed. Elena waved to her friend as she pulled out of the lot, wondering when she'd see her again.

That evening over dinner, Elena had brought up the subject of seeing Lamberto in the strange car at the funeral. She caught her mother off guard. "Why ... he hasn't said anything to me about it. I bet he borrowed a car, not wanting to be seen. He was there to protect you, Elena; I asked him to."

Not really buying her mother's story, Elena finished her meal and excused herself to return to her room. She turned on the evening news to hear the latest updates on Ralph Marinetti's murder. Seems there were ties to the Amato family in Cleveland. She had heard that name before, but couldn't recall where.

She turned off the news and climbed into bed, pulling the soft comforter up to her neck, thinking of Tony and how he was dealing with prison life. She turned to the nightstand and opened the drawer where she'd kept the gold bracelet. She rubbed her wrist, wondering if burying it had made things turn out for the better or worse.

The following week, Elena muddled through her classes. Her thoughts consisted of Tony and their romantic evenings together. She was so distracted in her drawing class that she missed the note Sean had passed to her. After class was dismissed, he tapped her on the shoulder, and she finally came out of her semi-coma. He made another attempt to invite her to join him for coffee.

Elena locked eyes with his deep blues and accepted, even though she wondered if she could be good company with her present mood.

There were no open tables in the coffee shop due to the lunchtime crowd, so Sean suggested they take their drinks out to an outdoor area a block away that had picnic tables shaded by large oaks.

Elena took a few sips of her coffee before she was ready to engage in conversation. Sean pushed his long bangs out of his eyes and started the conversation. "So, how's your final big project coming along?"

She hadn't even started her final project, but didn't want to confide in him. She had turned away in silence when out of the corner of her eye she caught sight of a cardinal that landed a few feet away.

Sean, realizing he may have started on the wrong foot, changed the subject and remarked on the cardinal — how they were regarded as signs or messengers from the other side.

His remark quickly caught Elena's attention, and she gave him a surprised look. It was the same thing her grandmother had told her about messengers and signs from the other side. *Was he superstitious or spiritual by nature?* She surely never would have taken him for one who believed in these things.

Their conversation flowed easily as they talked about paranormal events. She told Sean that, being Italian, she grew up with many superstitions.

Glancing at her watch, Elena said she had to be on her way as she had a study group this afternoon. It was a lie, but it didn't work to stop Sean from pushing further. He said he also had one and would love for her to join him and a few others at Mill Creek Park.

Hearing those words, Elena felt a chill rush down her spine. *Coincidence?* She glanced up at him and couldn't quell the few tears that began to well up in her eyes.

"What's wrong? Did I say something to offend you?" Sean asked.

"No ... it's nothing wrong — it's everything right."

Epilogue

2025

Elena sat at her kitchen table, hearing the soft hum of the ceiling fan turning lazily overhead as she watched *Youngstown's Days Gone By* on YouTube. The channel had become a quiet ritual of hers — an open window into a city she had left behind but never truly escaped.

The day's episode mentioned that several aging buildings on Market Street were scheduled for demolition. One of them was the old Rock Solid jewelry store.

Elena's breath caught.

She hadn't thought of that building in years. Not really. Not in a way that allowed memory to surface fully. But now it all came rushing back — the late spring of 1976, the weight of a gold bracelet in her hand — the one she had buried that night, hoping everything would change.

Another lifetime. Another world.

She had written to Tony more times than she could count while he was in prison. Every letter came back unopened. When word reached her that he had died at seventy-two, something in her had quietly folded in on itself. Not broken —just … sealed.

Life had gone on, as it always did.

In 1979, after earning a degree in art from Youngstown State University, she married Sean Dutton. They moved to Florida after her parents passed within months of each other. For decades she taught art in Fort Myers, filling classrooms with color and laughter. Sean had been kind, steady. When pancreatic cancer took him two years ago, she mourned him deeply. They'd had a good life, even if it had been a quieter one than the firestorm of her youth.

Now retired, Elena spent her days with a book club, volunteering at the Oceanside Art Museum, and walking the beach near her condo. It was a gentle life. A peaceful one.

But peace didn't erase memories.

She watched the video until the end. Demolition would begin soon.

By that afternoon, she had booked a flight to Youngstown. The decision came with surprising calm. She would visit her parents' graves. See Pam in Pittsburgh. Say goodbye to a few ghosts that had lingered too long.

And perhaps … retrieve something that had waited nearly half a century.

The October air in Youngstown carried a familiar chill. At the airport rental counter, she chose a small economy car and drove toward Market Street, her heart beating faster with every mile. The city had changed, but not enough to make it unrecognizable. Old storefronts still stood like aging sentinels, holding stories in their brick and mortar.

She stopped at Hanson's Hardware and bought a small trowel. It felt oddly ceremonial, carrying it to the car.

When she reached the jewelry store, a few of the walls were already gone. Two bulldozers sat silently during the workers' lunch break. Dust hung in the air like a memory refusing to settle.

She parked in the rear lot near a green dumpster and stepped out slowly.

Forty-nine years.

The spot was still there — just beyond the old streetlamp. Her hands trembled slightly as she knelt and began to dig. The earth was packed tight, stubborn with time. Then, at last, the trowel struck something solid.

She reached down and pulled free a tarnished gold bracelet.

For a moment, she simply held it, brushing dirt away with the edge of her sleeve. When she lifted it into the sunlight, the metal caught the light and shimmered as though no time had passed at all.

A laugh escaped her — soft, disbelieving. "Still beautiful," she whispered. She slipped it onto her wrist. As she turned back toward the car, something made her stop. A sensation more than a sound. A pull.

The back window of the remaining wall reflected the sky — and within it, a figure.

Her breath hitched.

Tony stood there, just as he had in 1976. Young. Unchanged. A red rose in his hand. He smiled — not with sadness, but with a kind of quiet peace she had never seen in him before.

Elena stepped closer, tears blurring her vision. She lifted her hand to the wall. For a heartbeat, it felt as though the years between them vanished.

Then the reflection faded and only the empty shell of the building remained. She stood there for a long time, the bracelet warm against her skin. And for the first time in decades, the memory of Tony didn't ache. It settled gently inside her — no longer a wound, but a chapter that had shaped her.

"Goodbye, Tony," she said softly. "Thank you … for loving me when we were young."

A breeze moved through the broken walls, stirring dust into the sunlight like drifting gold.

Elena returned to her car and sat for a moment, looking at the bracelet on her wrist. It no longer felt cursed. It felt like closure. Like something finally returned to its rightful place.

As she drove away, she didn't look back in sorrow. Only in gratitude.

Some loves were never meant to last a lifetime. But they could last long enough to change one.

And that, she realized, was its own kind of forever.

The End

About the Author

Lorraine Carey is not only a paranormal enthusiast but has had many unexplained events in her lifetime and has been inspired by these events to use as a focal point in her fiction novels. One of her YA Novels won a Silver Award from Reader's Favorite and was a finalist in the Wind Dancer Film Contest. As of current, she has fourteen published novels, three being co-authored, and has works included in four anthologies. Her genres mainly consist of the paranormal, but also include thrillers, romance, and erotica. As a veteran teacher, Lorraine began to write for Young Adults with the hopes of inspiring young readers. Currently residing in Florida, her retirement has given her more time to write when the spirits are willing.

If you enjoyed my novel, I'd love a review on Amazon or Goodreads. Thank you.

You can also find my other novels @
https://www.amazon.com/stores/author/B00ELQBUHQ